I love historical novels, and
tion Jonah is a fast-paced, act
to the continent of Africa wh
a romance, faith and crime-dr............ ....
two unsuspecting parents when their child is kidnapped by a
crime syndicate. You won't be able to put it down!

—FLOYD McCLUNG
All Nations
Cape Town, South Africa
www.floydandsally.org

The tale spun by Elisabeth is both shocking and heart-
warming. To kidnap or keep a child from his or her birth
mother or adoptive parents is to deny that child's funda-
mental human rights—to security, to a family, and even to
survival. But the response of the community to the crisis was
quite extraordinary. No one can fail to be touched by the
way in which such varied groups came together, so quickly
cutting across age-old divisions of race and religion in an
effective outpouring of common humanity. This is a story in
which near tragedy is turned into a triumph of the human
spirit.

—JEREMY POPE
Commissioner, New Zealand Human Rights Commission
Komihana Tikanga Tangata

A devout family caught in the crossfire between forces of
good and evil; persevering faith; community involvement;
supernatural intervention by God; ultimate triumph of good
over evil. These elements are vividly described in a sympathetic and intense manner. The author succeeds in conveying
a very positive message, without ever seeming to sermonize
or moralize.

—DR. VÉRONI KRÜGER
President
The Word for the World Bible Translators
www.twftw.org

Operation Jonah should not be dismissed as fiction. It is a true story that shows the power of unity. When an evil invader abducted a baby from an innocent family, a social bond that knows no skin color, religion, or social status defied all odds to find and return the baby to the parents. Justice reigned and virtue triumphed over evil as a direct result of people uniting for a moral cause. Elisabeth Miller has drawn from her rich experience of living in Africa to paint a picture of how life is experienced in an African context. This novel is a must-read for anybody with a passion for justice and honesty.

—Mvula J. Mvula, B. Th., M.A.
River of Life Evangelical Church
Malawi and Mozambique

Operation Jonah is a fast-tracking account of events that went horribly wrong in Africa. This surreal drama contains the elements of a tragedy and inspires the reader to move beyond empathy to courageous personal involvement on behalf of somebody in need. The book will keep the reader intrigued and spell-bound.

—Rev. Dr. Jan (John) Grey
Minister and Itinerant Evangelist
Australia and South Africa

OPERATION
jonah

Psalm 34 !
God is good. He gave us
the "Sign of Jonah" – Praise
be to His Name !
love
Julia (alias Debra)

ELISABETH
miller

CREATION
HOUSE
A STRANG COMPANY

OPERATION JONAH by Elisabeth Miller
Published by Creation House
A Strang Company
600 Rinehart Road
Lake Mary, Florida 32746
www.strangbookgroup.com

Unless otherwise noted, all Scripture quotations are from the Holy Bible, New International Version of the Bible. Copyright © 1973, 1978, 1984, International Bible Society. Used by permission.

Design Director: Bill Johnson

Cover design by Amanda Potter

Library of Congress Control Number: 2009932989
International Standard Book Number: 978-1-59979-910-0

First Edition

09 10 11 12 13 — 987654321
Printed in the United States of America

CONTENTS

ACKNOWLEDGMENTS

This book is another example of teamwork.
A big thank you to all who over the years generously contributed
memories, facts, impressions, ideas; expert technical, writing, and
design advice; moral, spiritual and financial support.
You know who you are.
Without you this book might not exist.

About the Author and Her Work

Miller's writing is not dissimilar to her cooking. Possibly a reader will claim to recognize a character or a landscape in *Operation Jonah*, as a connoisseur might insist he saw the recipe of her chicken curry in one or another exotic cook book. Neither might err entirely. Observing, sampling, analyzing, dissecting, mixing, and compounding are common tools used by writers and chefs alike.

Elisabeth grew up on a small farm in Germany. She joined Youth With A Mission and worked primarily in Africa. She claims this continent is so fast and varied, it must be tasted, smelled, seen, touched, and heard: The food, the sweat and the rain, the sunsets, the wire-haired children, the a capella choirs. She proposes you sit with precious African friends around smoky fires and exchange tales from the heart. Before you know it your presuppositions will be challenged and your desire to make a difference to those who suffer will be reinforced.

Elisabeth has explored the continent in public buses, crossed crocodile-invested rivers on dilapidated barges, dodged landmines, and found herself on the wrong side of a gun barrel several times. She has experienced the power of faith to instill hope and inspire the courage to tackle Africa's oppressors: fear and apathy, poverty and disease, injustice and abuse of authority. *Operation Jonah* teases your imagination with images of ripe mangoes, squawking chickens, potholed streets, and gentle, caring people. And beyond it a Creator who intervenes on behalf of those who trust in Him.

TO CONTACT THE AUTHOR

el.ywamafrica@gmail.com

Chapter 1
NIGHT RAMBLINGS

F INALLY THE RAINS let up. Rufus was cramped and sick of waiting. They had been holed up for hours, their car hidden in an unused driveway.

He cursed and slammed his hands on the steering wheel. Women! Great to look at, useless at a job! He was tempted to slap her, as he had slapped scores of other females, black and white, during his forty years of hard life. What was there for her to cry about? Never in a million years would he believe the claims she had made about having killed someone. She was too soft even for this job. He should have trusted his instincts. Now she was a liability. He cursed again and shot her a scowling look. "Pull yourself together, woman!"

"I'm trying," she snivelled in the backseat.

Rufus desperately needed the new car and money promised to him for this job, and jobs that paid this big were as hard to find as a striped leopard. It was high time to get this show on the road.

"Think of your sweet lover boy," he said. "He'll get the child with or without us. You heard him. He'll stop at nothing. Don't wanna be around when he hears you were too chicken. Will be no tea party, I promise you that."

The woman dabbed her eyes, seeming to agree with him but refusing to admit it.

"I hate this," she spat. "I should have never agreed to this. Three days I've been stuck with you foul-smelling brutes! You two haven't washed or changed your clothes once during this whole time we've been sitting in this rattle trap."

One of the lights inside the house they had been watching went out. Rufus looked at his partner, a baby-faced, tall youngster whose baseball cap barely covered his shaven scalp. "We got to go in now. Waited too long already." He turned to the woman. "Let's go over this one last time. All you do is knock at the gate and call their names. Tell them you need help. Tell them you are hurt. Tell them whatever you must to get them to unlock the gate. Got that?"

"Yes."

"We'll keep out of sight at first, but we'll be in as quick as lightning." He looked hard at the woman and at the young man, whom she had nicknamed Baldy. Both nodded.

"We pull the guns. In this light they won't know they're fake. I'll knock out the watchman. Baldy and I will tie up the adults." He briefly lifted one hand, holding handcuffs, then the other, which was holding rope. "The little girl should be fast asleep. If not, you pacify her. Got the sweets on you?" She nodded.

"Wanna keep the noise down. Should be no problem, thanks to the rain. We grab sonny-boy baby, the phones, and car keys. In and out in less than five minutes, I reckon. Cross the border, hand over the child, collect the money. Easy. Let's go."

He opened the door to get out. The woman started to weep again. Bloody white woman! There she sat, stalling and wiping her eyes. They had wasted too much time already. Apart from the outside security lights, the inside of the home was now in darkness.

"Come off it, woman!" he cried. "Let's get this job over and done with. It's now or never!"

"I can't do it," she whined.

"Suit yourself. We go it alone. More money for us. Ready, Baldy?" The younger man nodded.

Glad to be the decision-maker again, he turned to the woman. "Get behind the wheel. Soon as we're in, you drive up to the gate. Keep the engine running and two doors open. Be ready to take off the moment we touch the car. Can you at least do this much?"

She nodded.

"Let's get cracking." The two of them stuffed the ropes into their pockets, grabbed the handcuffs and toy guns, and ducked out into the road, ignoring the pouring rain.

Baldy hid behind a bush while Rufus picked up a stone and banged it against the gate. Dogs barked. After a while, the whites of a watchman's eyes appeared in the square peep-hole of the gate.

"What's up?"

"Need to speak to Mr. Warrington."

"Gone to bed."

"Must speak to him. Now."

The watchman just stared at them. Other dogs in the neighborhood joined the barking.

"This time of night?"

"Very important. Urgent business. Can't wait. Just tell him."

The old watchman dragged himself off towards a window at the end of the house to deliver the message. Five minutes later the lounge lights came back on. The door opened and Scott Warrington, a blond paraplegic in a wheelchair, appeared on the veranda, dressed only in a pair of trousers and spectacles. He peered across the veranda toward the gate.

"What's up?"

"Mr. Warrington?"

"Yes."

"I must talk to you."

"About what?"

"Business."

"I am not doing business."

"But I must talk to you. Please."

"Come tomorrow morning at nine." Scott Warrington turned his wheelchair around and closed the door. After a moment the house lay dark, but the dogs kept barking. Two hours later a sleep-deprived neighbor, fed up with the ruckus, fired his shotgun in the air. The trio sped away and the dogs finally settled down.

After that, the night returned to normal. The Warringtons were blissfully unaware they had narrowly avoided a kidnap attempt.

chapter 2
HEARTS AND FLOWERS

S COTT WARRINGTON AWAKENED from his world of dreams. With a sense of wonder he realized that the thundering tropical rain had finally stopped.

He fished for his glasses and inspected the ceiling for water damage. None. Thank God. He had lived all but two of his thirty-five years in Africa, but never had he experienced torrential rains like here in Mondawa, a small landlocked country leaving behind the excesses of dictatorship for a semblance of democracy.

In another area of the country, an entire mountainside had collapsed due to flash floods, burying villages and fields in its wake. Hundreds of people had died. Scott was thankful that their little house was solidly made of burned brick and had survived the worst of it.

Rolling over, he surveyed the pleasing form of his still-sleeping wife, Debra. He felt the luckiest man on Earth to wake up every morning beside such a beautiful and intelligent woman, five years younger than he. He was about to trace her blond hair and sensuous jaw line when his brain kicked in. Today was not just any Saturday, but Valentine's Day.

He slowly pushed himself up in bed and eased his body into his wheelchair. Due to a diving accident when he was seventeen, Scott was paralyzed from the waist down. Try as he would, he couldn't prevent the squeaking of the chair's rubber tires as he moved across the room. Debra insisted on leaving the bedroom doors ajar so she could hear every cough and yawn of their two children. For once Scott appreciated that he didn't have to open the door and risk more noise.

In the lounge, he retrieved the garden scissors from behind a ceramic flowerpot where he had hidden them the night before and let himself out on the porch. Their simple rented home was close to Kasiki village, nestled between a small tropical forest, a wooded mountain, and a river, which was swollen to its limits. The normally calming effect of the gurgling water had changed to a frightening roar. Scott made a mental note to inspect the fence in the near future. Children are inquisitive and can wander into danger when least expected.

The outside air, although fresh, was heavy with the blended scent of wet foliage and wood smoke from a village cooking fire. Having moved north from their native South Africa, the Warringtons appreciated the year-long display of blooms in their adopted home and the absence of morning frost. Scott spotted some dark purple bougainvilleas and sludged his wheelchair across the waterlogged lawn, passing a swing and a sandbox. Garu, their Rhodesian Ridgeback, emerged from a small opening in the garage door wagging his tail, racing around the wheelchair, and barking an enthusiastic welcome.

"Quiet, boy. Don't want to wake them just yet. Go to basket!" Instead, the brute followed his master across the garden, chasing rivulets of water falling from the creeper every time Scott touched and snipped at the thorny bougainvilleas. He added some canna stems to the wet pile of blooms across his lap and headed back to the house, tracking mud all the way. When he noticed what he'd done to Debra's tidy floor, Scott grabbed a rag and quickly mopped up.

If Debra had noticed her husband leaving, she didn't let on. He touched her nose with a wet bloom.

"Happy Valentine's Day, sleepyhead," he whispered.

She grinned with pleasure and yawned. "Hmm. You remembered. Sweet of you." She drowsily sat up and yawned again. As she reached out to hug him, she opened her eyes a fraction.

"Yuk. You are sopping wet. Go change."

Scott shrugged and suggested Debra, he, and the children shower outside under a hosepipe for the fun of it, but she wasn't game. As Debra wiped water from her husband's forehead and glasses, he embraced her, caring nothing about getting her wet or abusing the flowers in his lap.

"Go away, wet toad," she teased. "Clean yourself up. Then I'll hug you. And darling, please find a bucket or something for the flowers." Faint noise from the adjourning room indicated the kids were awake. As she scrambled from the bed to go next door, Scott called after her.

"A hug won't do it."

"Huh? "

"Only a proper kiss transforms the frog into a prince."

She laughed and disappeared.

chapter 3
STREET TALK

In Kasiki village, the squawking of chickens and the singing of birds had already signaled the beginning of a new day. Dutiful wives were up early, squinting against the biting smoke of the cooking fires they stoked. Most were indifferent to it being a Saturday and totally unaware that elsewhere in the world on February 14 people went to great lengths to express romantic love. The twigs and logs they had collected high up in the mountains and carried on their heads to their homes were green and wet, making it difficult to cook their meager meals. Even in times of hunger, husbands insisted on warm bath water.

One of them, Yusuf, threw open the shutters, which were locked securely every evening. After his bath, he downed a cup of tea and left for work in the market, where business flourished even in times like these. People exhibited their wares as much under the open sky as under old tarps, tin roofs, and tacky plastic sheets. He loved markets, where every single day fellow Africans would drop by, haggle over the price of produce, exchange news, and visit with each other.

"Jambo, Baba Chege," he addressed the older man respectfully, as he emerged from his home, carefully stepping over puddles. They often walked to the market together.

"Jambo, Baba Yusuf. You are smart, rolling up your trouser legs in this soup." He pointed to the soggy surface of the road. Both men wore sturdy sandals made of old car tires but still struggled for traction in the slippery mud.

Yusuf noticed his neighbor seemed troubled that day. The old man smiled, but the lines on his weathered, coal-black face hinted at the concerns of a worried heart. Yusuf waited respectfully before probing to see what was wrong. Finally, he took courage and asked.

"These are bad times, bad for everyone," Chege sighed. "The floods. The economy. People are hungry. Many people steal. Some use guns."

Yusuf fingered his grey beard, thinking of the wave of break-ins and increasingly violent robberies in and around Kasiki. Thugs had little difficulty recruiting hungry men to carry the loot from ransacked homes. The police were little help. Victims or witnesses usually had to fetch the police to investigate a crime, and stolen items were rarely recovered.

"At least it has stopped raining. Maybe some crops can be salvaged. Imagine the humiliation if we needed to ask the missionaries for food."

"Yeah. They are good people, but we can make our way."

Yusef paused to think a moment. "I like that Mr. Warrington. He got legs, but they are empty. His car is strong. He drives well over these bad roads, him being a cripple."

Chege laughed.

"What's funny?"

"The missionary with empty legs. Drives like the wind. Here one moment, gone the next. Don't know how, with those legs. The other day his car runs down the road, real hurry-like. My hearing goes slow. Heard nothing. Next thing I know, missionary stops and feathers flying in the air. Missus hops out looking all worried because car hit a rooster. I see it then. Almost naked, that rooster." The old man giggled like a schoolgirl and continued the story. "Shook itself and strutted away. People pointed at it and laughed. Missus then laughed, too. Jolly good show."

Yusuf was glad to see how much the old man was enjoying his own story.

"Mister wanted to pay. I say no."

"You did?"

"Yeah. Rooster makes good dinner, I say."

"Eh."

"But mister says no good for dinner."

"Why not?" asked Yusuf.

"'This rooster is tough,' he says. 'Surely you can see that, Baba.'"

The two men laughed and slapped each other's open palms.

"Chege," Yusuf said, "the missus, she drive just as fast, sometimes with those two white-haired children in the back."

"What? She drives too?"

"Yeah. She drives to the market sometimes. Good woman, she is. Always friendly, always asking about my family. Generous, too. She brings a big basket. I help her get what she needs. She happy; I happy. Never met such a fine white woman."

The two men arrived at the market, which was stirring to life.

The stands had way less food than usual, but Yusuf saw mangoes, tomatoes, fish, and green vegetables, impregnating the air with a rich profusion of aromas.

A skinny dog scampered between the legs of customers, vendors, and crude tables. The two friends waved good-bye, wishing each other well. Even in these troubled times, their smiles were not labored. Their hopeful hearts would carry them through another day of hard work.

chapter 4

THE SNATCH

W HILE THE WARRINGTON children entertained themselves in the lounge, Scott tightened the last screws on the reassembled office chair. Debra, the last to emerge from the shower, looked it over approvingly. She had changed into a clean T-shirt and knee-length trousers. She plopped herself into the chair and swiveled around, her legs brushing lightly against Scott's wheelchair.

"Well done, my star fixer and mender."

Besides making the occasional cup of tea, Scott happily conceded the kitchen to Debra. But he enjoyed fixing gadgets, especially when this earned him Debra's praise and saved a few bucks. She willingly gave up a career in nursing to join him in his translation work in Africa. *Not many wives have that kind of heart,* he thought.

"Did you notice the power went off again?" he remarked. "Was the shower still warm?"

"Just about. Wonder how long it will take this time to get it back on." She turned toward the kitchen, muttering something about rain leaking into connections and causing shorts.

Across the room, against a case filled with books, he watched Jasmina, who was absorbed with her dolls. "Sit still," she chided, "while Mommy brushes your hair," obviously mimicking Debra. Since the arrival of her brother, Dominic, she tried to be so grown up.

Dominic was chortling, reaching for the shorts his mother teased him with. True to habit, Debra had turned this nappy-change into a time of exercise and light-hearted talk.

"Show Daddy how you can stand. Any day now you will walk." Debra stood him on his feet and briefly let go. He held steady for a moment, but as soon as he tried to move, his balance left him. Debra swiftly caught him and laughed.

"Look, your teddy fell over, too." With one free hand she scooped up Dominic's white teddy bear. "Sorry, Teddy, for knocking you over," she said and placed a kiss on the beloved teddy's cheek before setting it down on the changing table. She then guided the baby's legs into a pair of blue shorts and pulled them up over the child's bottom, tucking in his dark red T-shirt. Next she placed him on her husband's lap. "Here we go. Keep Daddy busy while Mommy fixes lunch." Her lips brushed the noses of both father and child and headed for the kitchen.

From a pile of children's books Scott chose and read out of the one about Jonah being swallowed by a big fish and spending three days and three nights in its belly. Jasmina lost interest in her dolls and joined them.

"Jonah was very afraid and prayed to God. What happened next, Jasmina?"

"God heard Jonah and the fish spitted him out."

"Spat him out. Yes."

Debra interrupted, asking if Scott wanted a jam or cheese sandwich.

"How about bacon and eggs?"

"No time," she said. "And also there is no power. Remember? We need to leave for the party shortly. "

Jasmina's face lit up. She clapped her hands and marched in circles.

"Birthday party. Birthday party. Me, too, birthday party."

"Yes, Jasmina," Scott said. He looked forward to taking his family from the village and its current misery. A few hours with friends while celebrating a child's birthday would certainly lift their spirits. "A cheese sandwich will be fine."

As Debra turned toward the kitchen, the dog started barking. Scott noticed her pausing to look out of the window.

"Visitors," she said and moved across the lounge. "Oh, boy. Did the dog cause trouble again?" she sighed. He heard her turn the keys and open the door.

Two men burst in. One of them was tall and wearing a baseball cap, the other one was middle-aged and stocky with thick, tight curls covering half of his ears. The eyes of the tall one quickly surveyed the room and paused at the phone. He yanked it from its mounting and hurled it against the cement floor. It shattered in all directions. He then ripped the connecting cables from the wall. The other man yanked the keys from the door and shoved them into Debra's chest. She staggered against the wall.

A sickening thought flashed through Scott's mind. Would he rape her?

Scott deposited the baby on the floor and spun around. "What the heck...? Get out!" he roared and grabbed the stocky attacker by the collar of his dirty shirt. He peeled him off Debra and crashed his wheelchair footrest into the attacker's calves.

Debra reeled as from a trance. She stared wide-eyed at some point behind Scott and screamed, "Scott, he's taking Dominic. Stop him!"

The younger man tried to squeeze past Scott's wheelchair, dragging the screaming toddler behind him. Scott shoved Stocky toward the door and wheeled around, cutting off the kidnapper's escape. He locked his arms around the criminal's waist and tried to restrain him.

"Hands off the child!" Scott barked. His assailant's cap fell off, revealing a bald or shaven head. The stocky, older man came to the younger one's assistance, trying to free him from Scott's grip, pulling and jerking until the wheelchair overturned. The bald guy broke free, clutched the baby, and started for the door. However, Scott's arms quickly locked around his knees. No matter how hard the man pulled, dragging Scott across the floor, he couldn't break the lame missionary's grip.

Meanwhile, Debra fought the bald guy, trying to free the howling baby from his clutches. Someone swore. Clothing ripped. A grey T-shirt fell to the ground. A booted foot slammed into Scott's face, sending his glasses flying. Suddenly Scott let go, upsetting the kidnapper's balance. Dominic hit the floor. Debra caught him under his shoulders and pulled him one way, while a now-shirtless kidnapper grabbed the child's feet and pulled in the opposite direction. Afraid of hurting Dominic in this tug-of-war, Debra let go. The bald guy stumbled, regained his balance, and staggered to the door, swinging the screaming baby by his legs like a sack of potatoes. Dominic's head crashed against a handmade clay flowerpot, which broke on impact. Baldy didn't flinch, and held on to the screaming toddler.

The intruders bolted from the house, crossed the lawn, and made for the river.

Debra dashed after them.

Scott lay in the midst of the debris like a discarded doll. His head and rib cage felt as if they were wedged in a gigantic vice. He wanted to believe it had all been a bad dream. But he knew it wasn't. He tasted something sweet. He swallowed and swallowed again. Then he realized this warm, wet, and sticky flow was his own blood. Scott raised his head and flexed the muscles of his arms to push his limp body into a semi-seated position. The blood came mostly from his mouth. He rummaged his empty pockets for a handkerchief, then grabbed hold of the bottom of his golf shirt and pressed it against his lips. Running his tongue over his teeth, he was glad they seemed intact.

While supporting himself against gravity with one hand, Scott ran the other over his bruised face and the back of his head where he felt the beginnings of welts and bruises. He probed his limbs through the fabric of his tangled and soiled trousers, relieved that he could not detect any misalignment where he had lost all sensation during his diving accident years ago.

His heart was still racing and his breathing labored. Scott forced himself to breathe as deeply as the pain in his chest would allow him. With all his strength he roared in rage, screaming for help and hoping their neighbor would hear and come to their aid.

Silence.

Then Scott heard an eerie howl in the distance.

"My baby. Give me my baby! Please, give me my baby!"

Debra!

Bile rose from the pit of his gut and befuddled his senses, trying to smother his spirit with a wet blanket of despair. *God, help us*, he prayed.

chapter 5

NEIGHBORHOOD WATCH

"DID YOU HEAR why the fried chicken shop closed down?" asked Aanish Patel. His host, Billy Summer, a forty-seven-year-old boyish and boisterous American, looked puzzled by the question but kept tying balloons to a huge "Happy Birthday, Michaela" banner. The place was swarming with excited children.

"Why? The place was always packed. Must be over a month now since it was locked up. What happened?"

"The usual—theft! Some of the employees even poured cooking oil into their rubber boots. Rebottled and sold it at the market."

"Never."

"Promise."

"Wow. People are getting desperate, eh?"

Aanish explained the combination of factors at play: the food shortages, not unusual just before harvest time, combined with the breakdown of law and order after the disbanding of the previous regime's control mechanisms, and growing corruption.

Billy began setting up folding chairs while Aanish, who had grown up in Africa, continued to rattle on.

"Security is getting real bad. Almost every night now homes are broken into. The police come the next day and write a report. The real crooks hardly ever get arrested, and when they are, they get out on bail the same day."

"It's bad, man."

"I'm keeping a gun by my bedside."

"You're kidding."

"I'm not. I suspect the crooks brief the police on which area they are targeting for hits, and it works. They stay away."

"Surely neighborhood watch is a deterrent."

Billy's daughter, Michaela, a bubbly blond preschooler, held on to his trousers. "Daddy, start the games now?"

"Soon, honey. We're waiting for the Warringtons. You don't want to start without Jasmina and Dominic, do you?"

13

The girl shook her curls, then raced off to join the other kids. Billy walked over to a table where soft drinks were set out. "What can I get you?"

"A Coke, please. Thanks." He opened a bottle and poured two glasses.

"Yes, neighborhood watch is a deterrent, but we are a new force in town, facing huge obstacles. When armed policemen join us on patrol, it's a bit better. But we are civilians and have no authority."

"What about the new aerials going up? At least communication is better now."

"Sure. With the mobiles we can soon reach people on the outskirts of town, folks like the Warringtons. I'm concerned for them being so isolated out there."

"Scott maintains that they are in no danger."

"That guy is one cool dude. The day they come to take his wallet he'll probably offer them a cup of tea." Both chuckled. "How long do you think it will be until they're part of the radio system?"

"Christopher White is working on it," said Aanish.

Just then, Billy's wife, Margaret, joined them, offering a bowl of crisps. The men thanked her, using her nickname, Marge.

"It's great to have Mr. White working with us. He knows how the locals think and what makes the authorities tick. That's invaluable. And he knows what he's doing."

"Who?" asked Margaret.

"Christopher White. We've just appointed him to head up neighborhood watch. He's lived in this town all his life."

They chatted for a while about the marvels of mobile phones. They were expensive, but proved to be a real asset in a country where power and phone lines were often down.

The children kept asking for Jasmina and Dominic. It was unusual for the Warringtons to be late. Margaret decided the children had been patient long enough. "Let's start to eat," she said.

chapter 6
ON THE RUN

THE KIDNAPPERS SLOWED down to catch their breath. The baby had been screaming himself red-faced when they wrenched him from his parents, but finally he ran out of steam. Now the boy was just whimpering. Good. It was tempting to sit down and rest.

Stumbling across uneven terrain in this mud was hard-going. Their trousers were soaked from the wet grass. Baldy's naked torso glistened with sweat. Rufus stepped out again, reflecting. Who would have anticipated such resistance from a cripple? And the wife was quite feisty, too. She kept going after them. Baldy had reached the fence and needed both hands free to scale it.

"Can't believe she nearly caught up with us at the fence," said Baldy.

"That's why I shoved her into the bushes. Should have clobbered her. Got up and came after us again. Stupid cow."

While Debra had lost precious time disentangling herself from the spiky bamboo shrubs that had lanced her bare feet, legs, and shoulders, Rufus picked up the boy and threw him over the fence. Baldy caught him and continued his flight while Rufus scrambled over. She must have given up by now. They should have gone in with guns blazing—real ones. But that other stupid woman had been adamant about not using real guns. And the fake ones, as well as their treasured satellite phone, disappeared with her and the car. The entire plan had become unhinged. She was supposed to rush the kid across the border. Now she was gone. But at least they had the kid. Too bad they forgot to check if the Warringtons had a mobile phone. If they did, they might already be calling for help.

Have to move fast. He swatted at the mosquitoes buzzing around him.

"We'll backtrack now, through the bush. Less likely to be seen." He had hoped to swipe the Warringtons' cell phone to contact their employer after the snatch. They needed new instructions. He hated this time of the day when the sun was high and hot. The stifling humidity after the rains didn't help. While their feet trudged on, his mind wandered. They had to get to the rendezvous point, hand over the boy, and move on to South Africa. All Rufus could think about now was getting back to the man who had hired them and collecting their pay. He could hardly wait to spend it.

chapter 7

SHOCK WAVE

THE SILENCE AROUND Scott was uncharacteristic for this time of the day. Even the birds had taken flight, it seemed. Yet in his mind echoed Debra's distant but eerie howl.

He must get up and help her, he resolved, and squinted short-sightedly toward the open door. He groped for his glasses. Finding them cracked but holding together in their bent frame, he placed them tentatively on his bruised and bleeding face.

He was alive and finally able to collect his thoughts. "Jasmina?" he asked hesitantly. No response. He must find her. He dragged his body over scattered toys, wrecked furniture, and debris. Eventually he reached his overturned wheelchair and righted it.

He spotted Jasmina peeping from behind a doorway.

"Jasmina, oh Jasmina."

Hesitantly she stepped toward her father. "Daddy?"

Scott gathered his little girl in an embrace, ignoring the stabbing pain in his chest.

"Where is Mommy?" she sniveled.

"They've taken Dominic. Mommy has gone after them. We must pray."

Jasmina folded her hands inside Scott's. "Dear God, help us get Dominic back. Be with Mommy. Protect them both. Amen." He held her a moment longer, then turned her head so he could look into her frightened face. "Now, Jasmina, please help Daddy and push the chair toward me." Jasmina complied, and Scott struggled into it.

When Debra returned home, her face was flushed and streaked with tears.

"They've gone!" she stammered, not noticing Jasmina reaching for her mother's hand. "What can we do? Scott, what can we do?" she cried.

Scott wheeled himself to the small phone table, fingering for the mobile phone they usually kept there in a leaf basket. A letter that Scott had thrown into the same basket the previous evening had hidden it from the kidnapper's cursory view. "What's the number for the police?" He started to punch in a code. "No, man! The batteries are dead." He flicked on the light switch. "And still no power!" He contemplated for a moment. "You and Jasmina get into the car! We must get the police." He stared at the space beneath the door handle. "Where are the keys?"

Debra remembered. "They took them." She rushed toward the bedroom. "I'll get mine."

Scott raced his wheelchair out the door and heaved himself into the driving seat while Debra threw open the gate. She grabbed Jasmina and got in with her in the back seat.

"Leave the chair, Scott, just go!"

"No, Debra. Pack it."

She grunted, folded the foot rests, jerked up the seat, collapsed the chair, yanked it around the car, and threw it into the back.

chapter 8
SOUNDING THE ALARM

FERNANDO SINGH WAS a huge, meaty man of Indian, Portuguese, and African descent. He normally looked wild and unkempt. But today he appeared even more so dressed in a grubby tank top, army pants, and unlaced boots

His shoulder-length black curls clung to his forehead and neck, which were streaked with sweat and dirt. On his Kasiki property, which had been turned into a building site, he supervised twenty or so laborers. It had been a difficult morning. Building materials had literally disappeared overnight again, and his best mason hadn't reported for work. In the absence of electricity, power tools and cement mixers were useless. After receiving a delivery of long gum poles, he spent thirty minutes helping the driver negotiate his muddy driveway and turn his truck into the road without swiping the fence posts. Just as he got the trucker out the gate, he turned and saw the Warringtons' red Land Cruiser racing toward him, horns blaring. Scott slammed the brakes.

Debra Warrington leaped out before the vehicle had properly stopped. "They've taken my baby!" she screamed and doubled over, clutching her stomach. Fernando stepped up to the open passenger window, glancing at Scott in the driver's seat. His friend's battered face had a death-like color, and his eyes stared out at him from behind cracked spectacles.

Fernando noted that his T-shirt was blood-stained, torn, and filthy. Little Jasmina in the back seat reminded him of a scared mouse. "Scott? Are you okay?"

Scott closed his eyes for a moment, took a deep breath, and in halting words, related what happened. Several laborers watched curiously and drew closer.

"They fled over the river? Which direction?"

"Debra?"

She eased into a near upright position and pointed to lower-lying ground, covered by dense bush, about 200 meters beyond Fernando's property.

Fernando, the grandson of a Sikh soldier, took charge.

"Malcolm!"

"Yes, boss," replied a short, young African.

"Take some men and go after them. Hurry." He turned to Scott. "Have you called the police?"

Scott shook his head. "No. Our phone's dead, the mobile, too. We're on our way to the station. Debra, get in."

Debra jumped into their Cruiser and slammed the door as Scott gunned the engine and tore away. Fernando dashed into his house to retrieve his shotgun. Should he call the police? No use, he figured. The Warringtons were already on their way to the station. It made more sense for him to go after the kidnappers. He leaped into his battered Land Rover, hoping to chance across two black men with a white baby. He did his best thinking while driving. The Sikh shifted down to get through a patch of mud, then accelerated in pursuit of the kidnappers.

chapter 9

PARTY CRASHERS

Billy Summers groped blindfolded amongst a circle of squealing children and amused adults. Animal sounds lured him to a potential catch, but just before he could lay hands on her, the girl hopped aside to begin her teasing afresh. Billy schemed how to lure the children closer when he heard the blasting of a car horn too close for comfort. He tore off the blindfold. The men rushed from the veranda toward the gate, which the family's uniformed security guard, recognizing the vehicle, flung open. The Warringtons' four by four roared in.

Debra Warrington tumbled out, wailing that her baby had been taken. Billy's wife, Margaret, rushed to hold Debra, who shook like a leaf in a thunderstorm. Billy ran over to the driver's side. Scott said they were on their way to the police. On the spur of the moment, he decided to stop at the Summers' party to let them know Dominic had been taken.

"Did they hurt any of you?" asked Billy, who couldn't fail to notice Scott's battered appearance and Debra's bloody shins.

Scott was about to dismiss the concern when Debra said, "Dominic's head got slammed into a flower pot really hard. I'm sure he has a concussion and maybe worse."

Margaret held her tightly and softly asked her, "And you? Are you OK?"

Debra nodded. "I'm fine. But my boy, Dominic...oh, Dominic," she wailed.

"Did they ask for money? asked Aanish, addressing Scott.

"No."

"Did they take anything else from the house?"

"Keys. House keys, car keys."

"What about money? Did they take money?"

"No."

"Did they say anything? Who sent them, why they are doing it? Anything?"

"No. It happened real fast."

"They must be after money," Aanish declared. "Even though you don't have much, you have well-to-do friends inside and outside of this country. I'm sure they'll want ransom."

Aanish's remark about "friends outside the country" sparked something in Margaret Summers's mind. She stared at Aanish, then turned to her husband, Billy.

"They'll take him out of the country. I'm sure of it."

"Marge, you could be right," said Scott. He stared at his watch and then at Billy. "There's a flight leaving at one. Don't let it go before you are absolutely certain he's not on it." He then turned to Aanish Patel. "Please, rush to the border and notify the guards. You should need less than an hour to get to Mindi."

Aanish just nodded.

"Step on it!" Scott commanded.

He had never heard Scott being so directive.

Margaret volunteered to contact neighborhood watch and look after Jasmina. Debra nodded, lifted the child out of her seat, and placed her into Margaret's arms.

Scott was already revving the engine when he thought of something else. "I need a mobile phone. Mine is dead."

Aanish reached into his pocket and dropped his phone into Scott's lap. "Take it."

Two minutes later, three screeching vehicles roared away from the Summers's residence.

chapter 10
A KEEN EYE

MART'S FATHER, A teacher, had fled Mondawa when he learned
that the teenage student he had seduced was expecting a baby.
The young mother named her baby Smart in memory of his
educated father. Like hundreds of girls every year, she dropped out
of school and became a domestic worker, toiling long hours for a
pittance.

Smart grew up with his granny, who also struggled to make ends
meet. He would have loved to go to school, but there was no money
for uniforms, notebooks, or pens. Instead, the eight-year-old had to
tend goats. He used his quick wit to learn the ways of the woods,
being careful to avoid dangers such as deadly snakes and leopards.

As on countless other days, Smart had been up since the first light
of day, sweeping around the huts, fetching water, and preparing a fire
so breakfast could be cooked. After a meager meal of white maize
porridge he opened the kraal and let out his goats. He kept a keen eye
on his granny's vegetable patch, which the goats loved to stray toward.
His hands and pockets were full of small stones, ready to defend this
treasured piece of ground. Earlier, heavy rains had washed away many
of her new spinach plants.

Smart grazed his animals for several hours in the wooded hills at
the bottom of the mountain, then moved them up higher, where the
trees were taller, giving him and his flock much-needed protection
from the midday sun. There wasn't much for the goats to eat, but it
was a better resting place and gave him a sweeping view. Leaning his
skinny back against a tree trunk, he scanned the huts and shacks at
the foot of the mountain.

This day he looked at the section of Kasiki village where Mr. Silver
lived. Smart knew his distant uncle was very rich. He owned several
taxis, trucks, houses, and plenty of cars. Some Kasiki people said
Silver could multiply money by magic. It must be true. Where else
could so much wealth come from? Silver was known as a cruel man,
beating and killing people who crossed him. Whenever Smart saw

him, he always had big men with guns following him. The boy now looked down at his uncle's compound and hoped they would never have to meet.

Smart's granny had taught him to count to twenty so he would know when a goat went astray. At night when sitting around the fire or lying awake on his mat, he bugged people to teach him more. Now he could count to one hundred. When he was bored, like today, he counted the cars, buses, and trucks parked in Silver's compound. He got past fifty and then was not sure which ones he had already counted, so he started again.

What was that? Somebody ran through the bushes toward Silver's place. *That's odd. A man running in the middle of the day?* He was followed by another man carrying something. Smart strained his eyes. *Now that's funny.* They had a child with them, a white child, in blue shorts. They stopped outside the perimeter wall, banging on a section overgrown with vines. Judging from the sound, they were banging against something metal. Presently they disappeared and then reappeared inside the compound. *Cool.* Smart had looked out on the house many times, but he never knew there was a back gate. *Maybe the child is sick and needs urgent magic,* he reasoned. *But where were the parents?*

chapter 11

SKY WATCH: BILLY AT THE CONTROL TOWER

THE CONTROL TOWER'S 360-degree view of the airport revealed several parked small commercial planes, as well as a DC 300. The controller watched his instrument panel and spoke into his headset while he searched the horizon for the small chartered aircraft he'd been watching on his screen.

"Flight three-eight-five, Charlie-Alpha-Romeo; please come in on runway fifteen and taxi to the parking bay at the terminal. Over."

"Charlie-Alpha-Romeo, we roger runway fifteen. Over."

"Welcome to Kasiki airport."

Even though the small plane seemed light as a feather on touchdown, the air traffic controller continued to watch it closely. Behind him the door into the control tower flew open and Billy Summer bolted in. Because the controller, who was wearing thick headphones, didn't respond to him, Billy pushed his face into the man's line of vision. The controller glared at him and continued with his work.

"Charlie-Alpha-Romeo, you're all clear. Park at gate one. You will be directed. See you at the tower. Over."

"Roger. Thank you. Over and out."

The controller ripped off his headphones and stared at Billy, who surveyed the runway and the sky. With exaggerated politeness, the controller addressed Summer in a way that conveyed his displeasure.

"Morning, Mr. Summer. Or is it lunchtime already? How are you?"

"Sorry, Gregory. Got a problem. A kidnapping."

"A what? You're joking."

"The baby son of Scott Warrington has been kidnapped and may be smuggled out by air. When's the next flight taking off?"

"In 55 minutes."

"You mustn't let it go."

"Says who? You're a preacher, not God."

"The police must search the plane first."

"So? I need authorization to hold a plane."

"Authority from…?"

"Police."

Billy was already halfway out the door when he turned around. "I'll bring it. Hold the plane."

"And, Mr. Summer, the regional police, not just airport security."

"You'll get it. Hold any outbound plane."

chapter 12
POLICE BUSINESS

A HUNDRED YEARS AGO the quaint colonial government offices and the police station must have been impressive. But after decades of neglect, only a bulldozer could pave the way for progress into the twenty-first century. Some said they symbolized the broken state of law enforcement in Mondawa.

The Warringtons pulled up to the front door of the police station. Debra threw open the passenger door and raced inside. The officer at the reception desk was reading the sports page of the national newspaper, his feet propped on the counter.

"Please help! Our son's been kidnapped!"

The officer, peeved that this foreign woman hadn't greeted him properly, utterly ignored her.

Debra, scorning his petty protocols, snatched away his paper. "Get up and help us!" Her shouts echoed through the building. A door opened and a tall, burly officer with prominent stripes on his shoulders appeared, a pen in his hand and a pistol in his holster. He introduced himself as Inspector Kulaka and invited Debra into his office so he could take her statement.

While Inspector Kulaka searched his desk drawer for a ruler, Debra heard her husband's voice just outside. Somebody must have helped him up the stairs leading into the station. The door opened and Scott joined them in the grimy room where termites had destroyed several boards in Kulaka's office ceiling. Traffic fumes, mold, and water stains had ruined the rest.

Debra made the introductions and waited in torment while Kulaka carefully drew lines into the margins of the paper. Letter by letter, Debra and Scott watched him print the date in block letters.

Scott was asked to spell his name and give his birthday.

Debra wanted to jump out of her skin. "Surely this paper pushing can wait. Shouldn't we be out there looking for our son?"

"Let me assure you that everything possible is being done to track down your child and the kidnappers. Let us first establish the facts.

You must understand that I must have a report before we can proceed. Now, let's start at the beginning. You said it was around eleven o'clock, at your residence in Kasiki village. Right?"

Debra, noticing she was biting her nails, decided rather to sit on her hands.

At one point in their hour-long interview, the officer noticed her wiping away tears.

"Are you all right, Madam?"

She nodded. "This is his feeding time. I'm still nursing," she stated as a way of explanation.

"Ah. Let's return to the task at hand. How long have you been in the country?"

"About four years," said Scott.

"For what purpose are you in Mondawa?"

"We are missionaries, translating the Bible."

"I see. Would you have your work permit on you?"

"No. Our passports are at the house. The original papers are filed."

Transcription of the Warrington's statement took over thirty minutes and was clearly a major effort for Kulaka.

"Inspector, please, will the police send out officers to look for Dominic?"

"It's Saturday, Madam."

"I know. But, sir, this is a kidnapping. Surely there must be a way to mobilize policemen in a crisis like this."

"That's why I need this report." He tapped it and placed the loose pages into a folder. "I shall get this to my superior officer right away. I expect to meet him later today."

Debra didn't have much confidence that this report would do any good. She left determined to find Dominic on her own if necessary.

chapter 13

NEAR MISS: KIDNAPPERS
AND MRS. SILVER

T HEIR RUN THROUGH the bush in the heat of midday left them panting, parched, and famished. Rufus hoped that when they got to the Silver compound, they would get a pat on the back and a nice, cold beer. All they got were cold stares from men carrying machine guns. Finally, one of them left in search of some water. While waiting, Rufus stood at the back door of the house, longing to go inside and cool off.

The kid in Baldy's arms was sniveling. From an ever-so-white face, which appeared a tad blue, stared button-like eyes. Something around his mouth twitched as if he were ready to bawl again. When a woman appeared at the door, Baldy stepped forward.

"Here's the kid," he said, thrusting his bundle toward the woman. She bent forward to look but refused to touch the child.

"And what are we to do with him?"

"Don't know," answered Rufus, still panting. "Were told to drop him off here. Big Boss knows."

The woman seemed puzzled but unruffled. "Did you talk to anybody on the road? Did anybody observe you?"

"N–no. Actually, maybe some women saw us. They were collecting firewood."

There was a racket at the front gate and Madam Silver hurried off to see what it was. She returned shortly, spitting mad.

"Get out of here, you two! Disappear and don't come back."

"But what do we do with the kid?"

Somebody threw Baldy a blanket. He covered the sleeping child and turned toward the back gate.

"But wait! How did they know you are here? This gate is well concealed. I can't believe you came that way during the day. Somebody must have seen you. Don't you go near it."

One of her men appeared with a set of keys. "Come. Nice and quiet," he intoned. They hurried after him to a section of the yard

29

furthest away from the gate, and out of earshot from the house. Baldy placed the sleeping child inside the opened luggage compartment of a white Toyota Camry.

"One of you, too," the guard demanded. Baldy climbed in and the guard closed the lid.

Rufus heard more commotion at the front gate.

"Quick, in here!" shouted one of the guards, pointing to the back of a black BMW.

Rufus climbed in and got the lid slammed on his head. It was dark and hot and scary, like being roasted alive in an oven. Nobody seemed in a hurry to release him from this annex to hell. They still hadn't had a drop of water for hours.

chapter 14
COMMANDO CHRISTOPHER WHITE

CHRISTOPHER "CHRIS" WHITE, in his mid-fifties, held a British passport, but he had lived most of his life in Mondawa. Several of his younger years he had spent serving as an officer for Her Majesty's special commandos in various African countries. He had studied to be an engineer and opened his own firm, which didn't leave him much time for his other vocation, farming, so his wife, Josie, was the primary manager of their small farm on the slopes of Kasiki Mountain.

Chris was tending to a juvenile kudu antelope that had been rescued from a snare and brought to the Whites for recuperation. He spoke gently to the scared animal as he approached to clean the festering wound and apply antiseptic ointment. Just then, he heard Josie hollering for him from the direction of the house. She ran toward him and thrust his new HFS radio at him, panting.

"Marge Summer. About a kidnapping!"

When he heard the story, Christopher White was sure the whole issue was some mix-up and would be cleared up shortly. But Josie wasn't as hopeful.

"I don't like it, Chris. A missionary child, kidnapped. That's not something that happens in Mondawa. I have heard of a childless woman breaking under the weight of desperation and shame and taking off with a small child she chanced upon. I have heard of ritual killings. But kidnapping in this country? That's a new one."

Chris was still contemplating a suitable response when the radio came alive again. Fernando Singh wanted to ascertain whether the baby had been found.

"Stand by. I'll be right back."

Chris made a call to all members of the neighborhood watch, alerting them to the kidnapping and asking members to stand by for possible action. He also asked if anyone had information on a report that the boy had been found.

Billy Summer responded from the airport. "I'm with an officer from the regional police right now. Sorry, the response is negative. I'll be back as soon as the situation changes."

chapter 15

THE HUNT: AIRPORT SEARCH

O N HIS DAYS off, John Whitfield, the South African Airways representative, liked tinkering on his boat. He was busy with that when he was summoned to the airport by a frantic phone call from Billy Summer, followed by another one from his ground staff. A sweep of the terminals, restrooms, aprons, hangars, and even departing aircraft was being conducted. He dropped his tools, rinsed his hands, and raced to the airport dressed in work shorts and a T-shirt.

An adult's ticket had been changed at the last minute to a child's ticket. Airline staff feared that Dominic Warrington, wearing a girl's dress, might have been smuggled on board. The plane sat idling on the tarmac, waiting for permission to take off.

As Debra Warrington searched for her child on board, Whitfield stood next to Scott and two police officers, staring up at the parked plane. He had permitted the search, hoping the Warringtons would be quickly reunited with Dominic.

"I left instructions to pressurize the luggage compartment," he told Scott.

"You think Dominic could be in a suitcase? Could he survive?"

"It will get cold up there. The flight is not too long and they will fly as low as they possibly can today. That will increase the odds of survival, but I can give no guarantees. Sorry." Whitfield checked his watch. The plane was seventy minutes late for take-off already. His Johannesburg office would not be happy.

Debra finally appeared at the gangway, looking defeated. She trudged down the stairs, holding tightly to the railing. Halfway down the stairs she paused, found Scott's eyes, and shook her head slowly. She was crying. The suspicious ticket had been bought by a woman who decided to travel with her grandchild rather than her daughter.

Scott's phone rang in his lap. He snatched it up, listened for a moment, and in a voice heavy with disappointment said, "No. So far, no sign of him."

chapter 16

CONFRONTATION SILVER

MALCOLM BURST INTO his boss's house as Fernando finished another phone call, sounding the alarm about the kidnapping.

"Bwana. Come quickly. The baby has been taken to Silver's compound."

Grabbing his shotgun and neighborhood watch radio, the Sikh and a few of the men hurried to the truck. Fernando sped off, scattering startled chickens.

Fernando had met Silver just once. He knew the man had friends in top positions and was undoubtedly a crook. He also had a dubious reputation as an evil witchdoctor. There were wild stories of fatal beatings of those who incurred his anger. Some people swore they became rich overnight after Silver performed certain ceremonies with their cash.

As they got closer to Silver's place, one of the men shouted something about a policeman and gestured down the river bank. Fernando slammed on the brakes and reversed.

"Good day, officer," he shouted toward the policeman, whose sweat-drenched shirt clung to his back and chest. "Looking for the kidnappers?"

The policeman just nodded and climbed toward them. His rifle hung over his back. "Did you see them?" he panted.

"No, but you are most welcome to join us. We are after them, too."

Malcolm opened the front passenger door and scuttled closer to Fernando, making space. The policeman seemed glad for the transport.

"Glad to have you with us, officer. I'm Fernando Singh. I live around the corner, next door to the Warringtons. What's your name, sir?"

"Constable Muhalo," the officer shouted over the roar of the engine.

"Malcolm, fill him in," Fernando instructed while their old Land Rover raced through Kasiki village.

Malcolm said he and his men had been combing the area minutes after the kidnapping. They ran into women who told them of two men heading toward the mountainside carrying a white child. Following their directions, the searchers found a herd boy who said he had seen the child being taken to Silver's house.

"Constable," Fernando asked, "will you confront Silver about the missing child, or should I do it?"

An expression of uncertainty and fear darted across the policeman's face. "No, no. I will. But let's first see what the situation is." He was a cautious man, and seemed comforted by the presence of the huge Indian.

They turned off the dirt road into a narrow track along lines of urban, low-cost housing. Fernando parked with two tires on the shoulder of the lane in front of a high enclosure made of corrugated iron sheets. Lazy smoke drifted from a smoldering fire on the side of the road. The rubbish was too wet to burn properly. He blasted his horn, jumped out of the Rover, and banged on the gate.

"What do you want?" a gruff voice barked from inside.

"See Mr. Silver."

"Not here."

"I don't care. Open up. The police are here, too. We are looking for a child."

"Wait!" The gate remained shut. People, amongst them a woman, shouted something behind the gate. Fernando stretched, trying unsuccessfully to catch a glimpse of the house behind the enclosure. A crowd of nosy villagers formed around the Land Rover.

Somewhere a tinsmith hammered away, making metal basins and buckets from canisters that used to contain donated vegetable oil. A shutter in the door the size of a saucer opened and Fernando and Constable Muhalo found themselves being inspected by suspicious eyes. The head moved and revealed a flowered headscarf. Then the gate opened the width of a hand. Fernando lunged forward and forced it open a little farther. Inside he saw three heavily armed men shielding a woman in an African sarong. All four people glared at him.

"I'm Mrs. Silver. Can I help?"

She seemed cold but civil at least.

"We are looking for a white child. We hear he's been brought here," Fernando said.

Mrs. Silver turned and headed toward the house.

Moments later Fernando heard the approach of a car. A white Mercedes appeared and slid between the Land Rover and the growing crowd. The gate opened momentarily and swallowed the car. Fernando and his men followed it in, but the bodyguards drove them back. Fernando caught a glimpse of Silver inside and two more guards stepping from the Mercedes. His staff and his wife briefed Silver as guards slammed the gate shut on their unwanted visitors.

Fernando hammered on the gate.

"Mr. Silver!"

"What do you want?"

"I must talk to you, please."

After several minutes of awkward waiting, Silver barked out instructions. The gate opened briefly to admit the Sikh and the policeman. Fernando glanced around the compound. The house itself wasn't so large, but the compound was. He was surprised to see the yard packed with well over fifty cars, minivans, and trucks. He didn't think Silver ran a workshop from here.

"We are looking for a white baby. He was snatched from his parents, Mr. and Mrs. Warrington, about an hour ago, not even two kilometres from here. We are told the child was brought to your home."

"No. There is no white child here."

Fernando experienced a sensation that reminded him of his hunting days, when he felt the object of his search was within range, yet remained unseen.

"Can we come in, please?" the constable asked.

Silver glared at him, then turned around and made eye contact with his wife. She nodded and led the visitors to the house. Silver and the armed men followed.

The curtains of the living room were drawn, filtering out most of the light and leaving the room looking sinister. Out in the yard the sun had been at its most blinding. Their eyes struggled to adjust, yet they weren't dreaming it. The place was packed with stereo systems and other electronic devices, most of them with naked wire ends dangling. The policeman shot Singh a warning glance. Just in time, Fernando caught himself before concluding the Silvers were hoarding stolen goods. Instead, he strained to listen.

Silver gestured around the room. "I told you. There is no child here. Now get out." The party stepped back into the blazing sunlight. "But don't worry, the boy has been found."

The announcement stunned Fernando. Was it possible Silver told the truth? That gangster certainly had sources unavailable to Fernando. "Where?"

"The airport."

"Are you telling me the child has been found at Kasiki airport?"

"That's right."

This was exciting news—provided it was true.

"Let's see." He stepped toward the gate and asked to be let out. The constable accompanied him. Fernando looked over his shoulder and caught a view of Silver and his henchmen huddling together in conference. The gate slammed shut. At his Land Rover he retrieved his two-way radio and managed to reach Christopher White, the chairman of neighborhood watch, who asked him to stand by. As he was talking, he noticed several of Silver's men leave the compound and join the crowd outside. The radio squawked. It was White reporting back. There was no sign of Dominic at the airport.

Fernando, radio in hand and escorted by the constable, marched back to Silver's gate and demanded entry. The gate was opened wide this time. "It is not true. They have not found a child at the airport."

Silver, with a mock grin on his face, lifted his chin and raised his hand slightly, pointing to the crowd outside the gate.

"Look."

Fernando spun around and saw several men rocking his truck. It's nearly impossible for mere men to overturn an old Land Rover, but because the track was narrow, Fernando had parked on the washed-out shoulder of the road. He knew it wouldn't take much to tip over the unevenly parked vehicle. At the same time, the crowd got more rowdy, taunting Fernando's men. The police constable tried to restore order but was flung to the ground by one of Silver's thugs. Fernando couldn't believe his eyes as he watched this armed law enforcement officer struggle to his feet, brushing the dirt off his uniform. In a composed voice and attitude, he spoke to Silver, who had joined the crowd, in the local tribal language. Either his composure or his address calmed things down. Whatever it was, Fernando was impressed by the constable's quiet strength of character.

Fernando Singh seized the opportunity and hopped into the Land Rover. His men, including the constable, were still climbing in, when he reversed down the dirt track. It was time to get out of there and call on a higher authority.

chapter 17

ON THE BORDER: PASTOR JABU

EWS OF THE Warrington kidnapping was spreading through the Mondawan countryside like an autumn grassfire. In a nation with few phones and fewer highways, people communicated as they always had—neighbor to neighbor, farm to farm, village to village.

Pastor Jabu felt privileged to have a phone at the mission house in his little border town. Not even government offices were connected yet. Workmen had no sooner finished the installation when the phone rang.

Strange, thought Jabu. *Who even knows this number?*

He picked it up and answered cheerfully, but like a cloud darkening the noon sun, his face to lost its shine and a frown replaced the laugh lines.

"A kidnapping, you say? Yes, we'll keep eyes and ears open. We will pray for the child's safe return."

Jabu slowly replaced the receiver, wondering what to make of the report Billy Summer had just given him. It sounded crazy. Why would anyone take a missionary's baby? For ransom? Unlikely. But then, strange things happened these days, even in remote villages like his, a stone's throw from the border. Jabu immediately called in the three oldest of his seven children and dispatched them with urgent messages to the pastors of his congregations. He then took his best suit from a wire hanger and shook out the dust. His jacket would hopefully hide the frayed cuffs of his best shirt.

He polished his shoes and dressed with care. Pastor Summer had specifically instructed him to present one of the small cards bearing the denomination's logo and Summer's address and phone number to the district commissioner. He said it would lend credibility to his report and speed up the process of alerting the officials that thugs might try to smuggle a kidnapped baby across the border. Jabu placed one in his pocket and hurried off to see the commissioner.

chapter 18

THE HEAT IS UP: KIDNAPPERS IN TRUNK OF CAR

RUFUS HEARD THE kid's muffled cries and was not surprised. It was unbearably hot where he lay on the carpet below the rear seat, and Baldy and their charge would surely be roasting by now in the boot. If the kid died on them, they wouldn't get paid. He raised himself slowly and peeped into the yard. Earlier there were lots of boot-clad feet trotting about, but now all seemed strangely quiet.

Ever so carefully, he opened the BMW door and crept up to the Camry. It took him just two minutes to break into it and pull the boot release. The moment he touched the back fender he gasped. What was that foul odor? Before he had half opened the boot the stench became so pungent that it sent the hardened criminal reeling. The kid was sick from both ends. Baldy had thrown the blanket on some of the vomit, but it was no pretty sight.

It took Baldy a fair while to focus his eyes and scramble out of the boot. After several greedy gasps for air he said, "About time. What took so long? Almost suffocated myself in that hot car."

Mere moments after gulps of oxygen reached the kid's lungs, he, too, revived and began to howl. Within seconds, Rufus and Baldy were surrounded by Silver's men and staring down the barrels of assault rifles.

"Shut up! Someone will hear you," commanded the lead guard.

"Hey, it's not us screaming. The only way to shut up that kid up is to kill him, and I don't suggest you do that just yet."

"Who told you to get out of the car?"

"Any idea how dangerous it is in there, parked in the midday sun? Take us to the Big Boss."

The guards stepped back and Silver appeared.

"What's going on?" he demanded.

Before Rufus could say a word, Silver shot him a hateful glance. "The police could be back, and I can't have you traipsing around here, now can I? Guard! Get the keys to that Toyota!" He turned to Baldy. "Take the kid!"

Baldy clumsily scooped up the baby, who was whimpering again.

With AK-47s thrust into their backs, Rufus and Baldy were marched to a Toyota double-cab pickup and shoved into the front seat. *None of this is turning out like it's supposed to*, thought Rufus, who suddenly worried about his own skin.

"Not in the front, you idiots," Silver snarled at the guards. "Only the driver."

The head guard motioned for Rufus to stay in the front.

"The other one in the back. Someone get that guy a shirt, any shirt. The kid on the floor."

A torn jacket was flung at Baldy. He grabbed it and hopped back into the truck, battling to put the garment on his wet body. He curled up on the floor beside the near-lifeless form of the Warrington baby, careful to avoid the gooey brown substance oozing from the child's shorts.

One of the guards tossed the keys to a surprised Rufus and ordered him to start up the truck. Rufus climbed behind the wheel. Silver came over and leaned on the driver's side window. His stare looked so cold it nearly froze Rufus's already faint heart.

chapter 19

FRIENDS LIKE THESE

INSTEAD OF DRIVING into the town center, Fernando had stopped at the dingy police office closest to Silver's residence. With Constable Muhalo at his side, he politely requested a search warrant for Silver's place. The station commander listened sympathetically but stated that he had no authority to issue one. Fernando wouldn't take no for an answer. Eventually the station commander phoned his superior, who reminded him it was difficult to get magisterial authorization on a Saturday.

Fernando riled, "Surely you're not waiting until Monday morning before requesting a search warrant?"

The station commander shrugged with upturned hands.

"Anything can happen to that child while we argue, and you do nothing!"

"Don't worry, Mr. Singh. I'm sure the entire situation will be cleared up before long."

"Don't worry? I told the state president about the kidnapping, and you are reluctant to interrupt the magistrate on a Saturday afternoon?"

The police officer gaped at him. "The president? He knows?"

"Yes, I phoned his office and the media right before going to Silver's house."

"Ehh, in that case, Mr. Singh, please allow me to make a call."

"By all means, sir, by all means."

Before long the officer returned. The inspector general was at a holiday resort, he said, but he had contacted the district magistrate. Authorization could be expected to be in hand shortly.

Thirty minutes later the search warrant came through. Fernando didn't wait to read the document. He grabbed it and hurried from the building, two constables following him.

Surprisingly, a crowd had congregated in the station's parking lot. Fernando recognized some faces and was happy to see they had come to lend their support to the Warringtons. Fernando was talking to a neighbor when Scott and Debra drove up in their red Land Cruiser. They were instantly barraged with questions and expressions of comfort.

"We haven't found Dominic yet," said Scott from behind the wheel. "We've got people looking and pressing the authorities for help."

While Fernando had a word with Scott, he observed Debra scribbling down some numbers on a torn piece of paper and asking a lady friend to make some urgent calls on her behalf. At least one of the numbers started with the country code for South Africa. The tearful women hugged and promised to keep each other posted.

Fernando and the constables headed for the Land Rover.

chapter 20

NO VALENTINES FOR IRINA

I RINA COETZEE THOUGHT she might be famous someday, but for her work as an artist, not as the focus of a years-long court and media circus. The South African press had alternately portrayed her as a principled, caring birth mother and a selfish career chaser unworthy of motherhood.

Two years of soul-searching and emotional battering left her depressed and self-doubting. Why did she get involved with Anthony anyway? Angry and hurt as she was toward him, she couldn't erase the memory of those exciting first days together. Anthony Castledyn's rock star looks and irrepressible charm took her breath away. Within days of meeting him, they moved in together, filling the nights with passion.

He was a qualified personal trainer as well as a bodybuilder but kept hoping for better paying work in the IT field. The trouble was, he never liked the jobs he found. He would quit after a few days, always with some excuse. Meanwhile, he kept borrowing from Irina and others, always promising swift repayment. Anthony's promises were as beguiling as his compliments.

Irina once dreamed of marrying Anthony, but he wouldn't think of it, even after learning that she was carrying his child. That was two years ago. Yet, the memory of the conversation in which she told Anthony she was considering giving the baby up for adoption was still raw.

"Give my baby to strangers? Are you crazy?" he spat. "How can you be so callous?"

Irina tried to explain that she was just considering adoption, but Anthony lunged at her, knocking over his chair.

"You care at all about me and how I feel about this?" he snarled. Then he stalked out of the restaurant, leaving her embarrassed and wounded.

Kitty van Rooyen, Irina's adoption counselor, got an unexpected visit from Anthony a few days later. He went to see her, ostensibly to learn more about the adoption process. During their contentious thirty-minute appointment, Kitty learned that Anthony himself had been adopted as an infant. She pressed to see if the adoptive parents had mistreated him. No, he conceded. They were good people.

"Why are you so against adoption then?"

"Because it's a selfish choice. I still don't understand how my birth mother—or any woman—could just abandon her kid. Early in my life I decided I could never trust a woman, and I still don't."

Irina knew nothing of Anthony's root issue with women. She had tried but failed to make their relationship work. Most of all, she felt helpless to discern his shifting moods. Out of the blue he had asked her to marry him. He could be utterly charming and affirming one moment and abusive the next. Anthony fought like a demon to have his way in any argument. Irina became increasingly afraid of his temper. As a casualty of her own parents' marital wars, she shuddered thinking Anthony might use her yet-unborn child as a means of getting back at her for daring to cross him.

Though not a particularly religious person, one night Irina sat on her bed weeping and found herself calling out to God.

"What am I to do, God? What am I to do? You know I want to keep this child. You know Anthony too. He says he'll marry me if I keep the child, but I don't trust him to care for me or this baby." Irina sobbed into her pillow. She regretted ever getting into this relationship. Their values were so different. He had told her that even if they married, he wanted to have nothing to do with her family. "God, you know I can't do that. Show me what to do." She could hardly breathe. She rummaged for tissues and blew her nose. Heart-rending as it was, adoption seemed the only right way to go. And nobody but she could make that call.

God had answered Irina's prayers and helped her choose a wonderful family for her baby. Debra Warrington, the adoptive mother, had gone to great lengths to be able to produce milk with the help of medication and artificial aids.

Being a qualified nurse, Debra was allowed to assist during the delivery. Beaming broadly, she handed Irina the slippery newborn. He was healthy and breathtakingly beautiful. She cradled him close to her body and grudgingly gave him up just long enough to be checked and cleaned up. While in the hospital, Dominic slept in Irina's arms. Debra, who had become like a sister to her, stood by to feed him and change his nappies.

Irina returned to her mother's house alone.

The day the court finalized the adoption, Irina held her son one last time. The parting was more difficult than Irina had anticipated. Excruciating pangs of loss threatened to crash over her like giant waves, thrusting her into a tumbling spiral of doom. Her every emotion screamed in fury against this unnatural separation, yet she forced herself to consider her child's future rather than her own feelings. Only then could she face another day.

As a parting gift for her son, she bought him a white teddy bear with a red sash bearing the words "I love you."

Scott and Debra Warrington's family was now complete. Within twenty-four hours of adopting little Dominic, they had left South Africa.

Irina had supposed that when the adoption went through, Anthony would let up on his verbal attacks on her. Instead, he stepped up his campaign, playing the role of the victimized father who had no rights to determine the future of his own son. He garnered the sympathies of low-life friends, lawyers, talk-show hosts, and activists. All chipped in to get a pound of Irina's flesh, trying with all conceivable means to prevent the adoption. She received lewd phone calls, demands of payment for products never ordered, terrible press, and summons to court—all in an effort to have the adoption order reversed. To her utter consternation, he won the case.

Irina and the adoptive parents were shocked. They swiftly launched a joint appeal. Week followed week of anxious phone calls, hurried legal consultations, home visits from welfare and legal departments, and much agonized prayer. The breastfed baby sensed his mother's tension and suffered from bouts of colic. Finally the case was settled and the adoption was confirmed.

But Anthony Castledyn did not give up. He found backers and launched a new court case—this time against the state. The constitutional court, in a landmark case, ordered the childcare act to be amended to consider the rights of unmarried fathers. The press had another field day, commiserating with Castledyn that his victory came too late for him and his child.

Nine days later, on February 14, instead of Valentine cards, chocolates, and flowers, Irina received a call. Dominic had been kidnapped.

chapter 21

HOT CARGO

RUFUS WAS LIVID. *There could be spot-checks by traffic police and here I am driving one of Silver's stolen trucks, with a stolen white baby inside.* What rotten luck!

Though no stranger to scrapes with the law, Rufus prided himself on his skill at avoiding the authorities. He survived the concrete jungles of South Africa by relying heavily on his wits. They would have to save him now. Near the major junction to Kasiki town, Baldy popped his head up.

"Keep down! Do you want the authorities to see you and that kid?"

Baldy ducked down but was dying to get off the hot floor of the pickup. It was making him sick. The kid, too.

"How much further? I can't take this much longer."

"Just lay low. We'll be at the safehouse soon. We can rest there, then hand over the baby and get our money."

Rufus hoped that one of the backup plans Castledyn had hatched would work out. He drove the Toyota pickup to a shack near the airport. Baldy holed up there with the kid while Rufus hopped on a taxi for the short ride to the airport.

Good night! When he walked in, the place was crawling with police and nervous airline employees. He couldn't ask one simple question without getting his ears chewed off about a mysterious kidnapping of a baby that morning. He almost expected to be handcuffed any moment. How in the world could word about the snatch have spread so fast? Rufus scanned the departure area. No trace of Castledyn's fancy girlfriend. She was supposed to take the child on the Saturday afternoon flight to South Africa. Rufus cursed under his breath and beat a hasty retreat.

He stopped along the road and used up the last of his money to call a satellite phone used by Castledyn.

"I've got the item."

"About time."

"Silver didn't accept the item. I've checked the airport. The SAA flight is about to board. Where's the courier?"

"She's here with me."

"What?" He knew it. That woman was trouble, but Castledyn didn't want to face facts when he should have pulled her off the job.

"Changed her mind."

"And?"

"You bring the kid across the border."

"It's not that simple."

"Why not?"

"It costs money, and you haven't come through on the second installment, remember?"

"Money for what?"

"Bribes, fuel, and road insurance. Accommodation along the way."

Silence.

"Hurry up. This call is expensive. We may be cut off."

"Borrow the money. Don't go to any public place. Drive through the night. Take turns at the wheel. Meet me close to the South African border. I'll be waiting for you." Castledyn gave him the name of a well-known watering hole.

Rufus was peeved that this guy was living it up while his own neck was on the line.

"And don't disappoint me. I've paid dearly for getting this item. You will not like the reception you get in South Africa if you fail."

"Are you threatening me?"

Castledyn ignored the question. "Oh, one more thing: I would prefer getting him alive." The line went dead.

Rufus returned to the bakkie. The kid was screaming again. Baldy wanted to know what Castledyn had said.

"He hasn't even asked about the kid."

Neither Baldy nor he wanted to touch the noisy, stinking rag bag.

"He's probably hungry," Baldy said. "And so am I."

Rufus organized some money and several packets of custard cream biscuits for the three of them. This mollified the screaming creature for a while. They couldn't afford to lose more time if they wanted to clear the border before six.

chapter 22

SEARCH OF SILVER'S PLACE

T HE WINDOW WAS down and Fernando's long hair flapped in the breeze as he led a speeding convoy of cars toward Silver's house. His thoughts were also racing. *Got to get there fast. No telling what they might do with that child.*

Two constables bounced on the back seat, exchanging fearful glances. Three hundred meters before they got to the dirt track leading into Silver's property, an oncoming white double-cab pickup appeared, moving at breakneck speed. The truck narrowly missed the Land Rover and other cars as it sped by.

"What the heck!" Fernando slammed on the brakes. The driver in the car behind him reacted just in time to avoid rear-ending the Rover. Without hesitation, he wheeled around on the narrow road, some intuition telling him to stop that double cab.

"Follow that truck!" Fernando shouted to the other drivers.

Some of the men in the other cars followed his instructions, but it took precious minutes to disentangle from the convoy. By the time they turned around and gave chase, the white pickup was well out of sight.

What a lousy road! We've got to catch them. Fernando's battered Rover careened on two wheels for a while, precariously close to the other cars. The moment all four wheels touched down, the Sikh floored the accelerator and sped off in the direction they had come from, leaving behind a cloud of black fumes reeking of exhaust and burned tires. Only now did he catch sight of his passengers in the rear-view mirror. Despite their black skin, both constables were noticeably paler.

"Sorry, gentlemen. I just had this sudden—" he tried to find the right word. "I just feel the child's in that truck."

"This is reckless driving," Constable Muhalo muttered. "You could cause an accident with bodily harm. Forget that truck. We are here to search a house."

Fernando slowed for a moment, pondering what to do. His gut told him to go after that pickup, but what chance did he have to catch them with his diesel-guzzling old Rover? *It's certainly not up to a high-speed chase. Best to oblige the constables and hope someone else can catch that white pickup.*

He stopped the Rover and flagged down the first driver behind him. It was one of the Warringtons' friends, someone he'd seen earlier that day. A good sign.

"There's a white double-cab truck up ahead. See if you can stop it. It may be hiding the Warringtons' baby. I've got to help the police execute a search warrant at Silver's house."

A crowd formed outside Silver's compound as soon as Fernando's convoy pulled up. He and the constables approached the gate and asked to see Mr. Silver. A few minutes passed before they were admitted and met by Silver himself.

"Good afternoon, gentlemen," he beamed. "Come in." The man seemed transformed since Fernando last met him.

One of the constables handed Silver the warrant. He studied it.

"A search warrant? I understand you are looking for a child. Very unfortunate affair. I told you before there is no child here, but look around, if you must." He led Fernando and the constables into the lounge. Six men remained with the cars.

Electronic gadgets were stashed in every available space: under the beds, on top of a rudimentary wardrobe, piled high on the floors. Most of the system components displayed poking wires, either ripped or cut. Decoders, DVD players, laptops, PCs, and cell phones littered the rooms, some of them expensive models.

"Surely, a thief's lair!" Fernando grunted under his breath.

"We are searching for a child. Remember that!" snapped Muhalo.

The search continued room to room.

"Do you see a baby? No. There is no baby. Now go!" Silver looked furious.

"Please be quiet," Fernando said. "We might hear him. He could be hidden somewhere here."

"Why would I want a child? We have more than enough in this country," Silver sneered.

The constables began opening potential hiding places, to no avail. When they had searched the last room, Silver and his henchmen herded the three men out the door.

"How about we search the cars outside?"

The officers seemed rankled by the suggestion.

"This warrant applies only to the house," Muhalo replied.

No sense pushing it with these guys, thought Fernando. *I wish I had followed that truck.*

chapter 23
HIGHER AUTHORITY

THE MOMENT HE set foot in his house, Fernando went straight to the phone. He placed three calls in rapid succession—one to the national broadcaster, a second to a leading newspaper in South Africa, and a third to Mondawa's head of state. The presidential palace staff put him on hold. The longer he waited, the more he wanted to give in to his choleric nature and throttle the bureaucrat at the other end of the line.

"Be polite and patient, now," he muttered to himself. "Unless I adhere to their stinking protocol, there's no way they will put through my call to the president." Fernando had worked with President Manukwa during his days in the construction business. Now the most powerful man in the nation, he was shielded by advisors, bodyguards, soldiers, and secretaries. He once was a common man, but now he insisted on being called "His Excellency, the State President Dr. Abdullah Manukwa." Power had a way of changing people.

When the president finally came on the line, he greeted Fernando Singh like the old business associate he was, which made it easy to brief him on the kidnapping and the eyewitness implicating Silver.

"I can't believe Silver would have anything to do with this."

"Well, if you were not president I would say there is convincing evidence to the contrary." Fernando winced. Being so upfront and noncompliant with an African leader could cost dearly. But he couldn't help himself.

The president paused. "Let me look into it."

"Thank you, Your Excellency."

Click.

Two hours later, Fernando received a call from the bureaucrat.

"Yes, *S-i-n-g-h*...Yes, I did call about two hours ago....Yes, I'll wait." Fernando drummed his fingers on the table.

The president came on the line. Fernando held his breath and listened.

"Fine, thanks....No, I think we were too late....The parents fear the child might be whisked out of the country.... Thank you, your Excellency. I shall expect the inspector general's call."

Fernando replaced the receiver and waited for the promised call.

chapter 24

A SUSPECT

A T THE POLICE station Scott squeezed his wheelchair into the pigeon-hole office. It was stifling hot. The door could no longer close, which improved ventilation but kissed privacy good-bye. Debra sat on a dilapidated chair, still wearing the same dirty, tear-stained T-shirt. She fidgeted and squeezed her husband's hand.

On the other side of the ancient hardwood desk, Police Inspector Makepe wiped the sweat off his forehead. His questions clearly showed Scott and Debra that he didn't grasp the concept of adoption. In matrilineal tribes, children almost always remained within their mother's clan when a parent died or chose to leave. Scott knew the Makepes of Mondawa formed part of a patriarchal tribe where family members belonged irrevocably to the father's clan. Giving or selling a child to anyone not closely related to the father was considered monstrous.

While Inspector Makepe seemed friendly and trusting, Scott struggled to convince him that even without blood ties it was OK to treat Dominic as their own.

"Mr. Warrington, you suggested the father of the child, Mr. Castledyn, a South African, is behind the abduction?"

"The biological father. Yes."

"But surely, a father who collects his small child from across several country borders, years before that child is able to help with the simplest of tasks, must be wealthy and quite desperate." He rearranged himself in his seat. "You insist that you are Dominic's legal parents. Forgive me, but I need to see those documents as soon as possible. Meanwhile, please tell me why you suspect Mr. Castledyn."

Scott thought for a moment and shifted his position. "The day the adoption was finalized by the court, Castledyn made an urgent legal claim to know our identities."

"He didn't know you?"

"No," said Scott. "He didn't. But the birth mother did. As a single mom, she could give up her child for adoption without the consent of the father."

"So, he wanted to get to know the people who were going to raise his child. That's reasonable, I'd say."

"The judge found Castledyn was obsessed to know the whereabouts of his son. He felt that the lives of Dominic and us, the adoptive parents, would be made intolerable if the biological father would discover who and where we were."

"Ahh."

"His application was thrown out," said Debra. "But Castledyn and his lawyer made a huge fuss, saying his human rights were abused."

"And?"

"An advocate was appointed as *curator ad litem* to represent Dominic since he is a minor," said Debra. "She came and visited our family here at Kasiki and recommended in her report that Dominic should stay with us. "

Makepe's eyebrows shot up. "But why? You are not related."

"Irina Coetzee, the biological mother, was not married," Debra explained. "She believed strongly that her former boyfriend would be an unsuitable father."

"And the authorities agreed?" the inspector asked.

"The courts checked out the biological father. They found he could not offer the child what we could," said Scott.

Inspector Makepe scratched his head. "Hmm, this is certainly a complicated situation."

Debra remembered something else. "The judge pointed out that Castledyn kept changing his contentions from application to application in order to suit the prerequisites of a particular court. He ruled that it could not possibly be in Dominic's best interest to grant Castledyn's request."

"However, he did achieve a change of legislation," Scott said. "The Constitutional Court ruled that unmarried fathers must be given a say in the adoption of their illegitimate child. Parliament must change the law within two years."

Inspector Makepe came alive again, his interest sparked.

"So the father came and claimed his child."

"No. Dominic is fully our child—as if he were our biological son. Nothing can change that, not even a change of the adoption laws. Until Parliament finalizes the change of a law, the previous laws remains effective. The change in legislation came too late for Castledyn."

Scott watched Makepe carefully, hoping he would be moved enough by their story to finally mobilize the police. He had seemed sympathetic after witnessing the destruction in their lounge. Scott had laid all their cards on the table, sparing no detail about the kidnapping and the efforts to find Dominic. Now he looked into Makepe's eyes and prayed a silent but urgent prayer. *God, make this man help us. Please.*

Chapter 25
NOISEBOYS

J AKE VERMEULEN BARELY knew the Warringtons but offered his
workshop in response to his wife's plea that Scott and his friends
needed a central place to meet and coordinate their efforts to
find Dominic. The main line of NoiseBoys was the repair and replace-
ment of car exhausts. They also installed alarms, changed tires, and
did other routine maintenance jobs. During working hours the shop
buzzed with the movement of vehicles and the blare of at least one car
radio above all the work-related banging and shouting. After close of
business on any Saturday afternoon, the swept and tidied factory-type
shed still smelled of engine grease but otherwise was as quiet and eerie
as a cemetery. Its central location made it a perfect gathering place
and command center.

Jake was a tall and well-toned Afrikaner. If given the choice, he,
like many other hard-working descendants of Dutch immigrants,
preferred sleeping in a tent at a riverbank to rooming in a five-star
hotel. To survive in this place, one had to be as tough as the land yet
always willing to lend a hand to a neighbor in need.

When the Warringtons pulled up, Jake rushed ahead of Debra
and retrieved the wheelchair from the truck, holding it in place while
Scott lowered himself into it.

Debra closed the doors, and Scott pressed the key-locking device.
Jake easily pushed him up the ramp into his workshop. A half-dozen
friends were there, eagerly awaiting word on the search for Dominic.

"Just give us a few minutes to get organized here," Scott said.

Jake hastily rearranged his office furniture to allow easier access for
Scott's wheelchair. He removed his swivel chair and offered Scott his
place behind the desk. "We have two lines," he said. "The fax machine
can also be used for calls. Dial zero for an outside line, triple zero
before dialing an international number."

Scott looked around the room, which quickly filled with people.
Not all of them were familiar to him. He recognized Rodney and
Darlene Archer, Christopher White, and Aanish, the Indian friend of

the Summers. He thanked them for coming and briefed them on the kidnapping. An eyewitness reported a white child being carried into Silver's compound. By the time a warrant was obtained, Dominic was nowhere to be seen. He was possibly whisked away in a white double-cab Toyota pickup, registration unknown. No plane from Kasiki airport or any other airstrip in the nation was cleared for takeoff without being first checked by police.

A hairy Portuguese farmer wearing thick khaki shorts, knee socks, and a floppy hat, cleared his throat and addressed Scott. "Got a demand for ransom?"

"No," said Scott. "Not yet anyway. May we know your name, sir?"

"Augusto Azolin. I don't like it that people walk into our houses and just take what they want. In the past, we quietly suffered the confiscation of our shops, houses, and lands. They may take our things, even if it's wrong," sweat ran from his brow and down his open shirt front, "but they must not take our children. It must stop. Now."

There was a chorus of affirmation and everybody seemed to be talking at once. Scott failed to make himself heard over the noise.

"Quiet, please. Let Scott speak," shouted Jake.

"Thank you, Mr. Azolin; thank you, Jake. Let me give you some background."

By then, more people had squeezed into the office and others strained to hear from the workshop. Scott told them the story of Dominic's controversial adoption and said there was a good chance that the biological father in South Africa was behind the kidnapping. That was news to most of the people present and explained why the planes needed to be searched.

"Scott, what are your main needs now?" asked Jake.

"Communication," answered Scott. "We need mobile phones, even though the network has many dead spots. Also high-frequency radios."

The Portuguese spoke again. "The radio signals are too weak to be much help. That's why we're building a new repeater station."

"What would it take to make it operational now?" Jake asked.

"I don't know, but I'll find out."

"Thanks. Let us know tonight."

"How about roadblocks?" Aanish asked.

"Great idea. But we need police presence."

"I'll try to organize it," Christopher White said.

Jake asked who amongst the group would be willing to form the first shift, starting immediately, even though police presence was not yet available.

The Portuguese farmer's hand was the first to go up. Seven other men followed his example. Jake suggested the eight of them meet outside the overflowing office.

As the men filed out, they collided with Billy Summer, who was hurrying to get in. His sweat-soaked shirt clung to his body, and his face was flushed and wet.

"Scott," he hollered. "Any breakthrough?"

"Not yet."

"I've set up an interview with NBC. Scott and Debra, you must go there."

"When?"

"Now. They began broadcasting the story and promised to repeat it every fifteen minutes. They want to interview you live."

Before Scott had a chance to respond, Billy ploughed on. "Also, we need to announce a reward. Then people are more likely to come forward with information. I pledge fifty thousand Kwanzos."

Others promptly responded, and soon 150,000 Kwanzos were pledged—nearly the annual salary for an unskilled worker. Scott prepared to leave, but Billy had more ideas. "We need a recent photo of Dominic. While I take Scott and Debra to NBC, somebody must find a print shop and prepare for the printing of several hundred posters before nightfall."

"This is Saturday afternoon," said Darlene Archer, a friend of Debra. "But I'll contact some print shops I know."

Scott, trying to get out of the room, caught a trash bin with his footrest and knocked it over. Debra tried to catch it.

"Leave these dumb papers, Debs. Let's go," Scott grunted, while people scuttled to let them through.

chapter 26
SOUTH AFRICA

CASTLEDYN HAD KNOWN the lawyer for almost two years, but had never experienced him this furious.

"I don't care one bit about where you are. No excuses. You get over here *now*! They won't stop ringing your doorbell, nor your mobile number."

"There's no network in this forsaken country for my South African phone. You're lucky to catch me. I just got the satellite phone back."

"Lucky? Did you say I am lucky?" The lawyer almost spluttered. "You got yourself buried in a huge truckload of trouble. By the way, your face is on TV again—not as a longsuffering father but as the main suspect in the brutal kidnapping of that innocent babe from the caring hands of his angelic missionary parents. You really messed this up."

The fat lawyer sounded dangerously close to a heart attack. And what was that about being on South African TV in connection with the kidnapping in Mondawa? He hadn't set foot into that country for the very reason of avoiding suspicion. It didn't make sense.

"I know you love your drink. I think you've had too much," said Anthony.

"Stop insulting me. Get here now! That's an order—and it includes your girlfriend."

"Impossible. We're several hundred kilometers from the nearest border post, and they close at nightfall. We had all sorts of complications when—"

"Don't you dare tell me those details. Hire whatever plane or parachute you must, but you better answer your doorbell as well as your phone on the very first ring tomorrow morning. Do you hear me?"

Click.

chapter 27

EMPTY PLACES

W HEELING HIMSELF FROM his study, where he had retrieved papers from the filing cabinet and a photo album from the shelf, Scott noticed Debra staring at the play corner in the lounge. He was about to tell her to hurry up but stifled the urge.

Instead, he wheeled himself to her side. She seemed unaware of him. He longed to reach out and enfold her. His wheelchair was a nuisance many times, and right now he really wished to be rid of it and gather her tender frame to himself. Instead, all he could do was touch her wrist and gently massage it. "Debra, my love."

Slowly her tension receded and her eyes focussed. After a while she responded, placing her icy cold hands between his for comfort.

"Tell me that this—" she pointed at the scattered toys, overturned and damaged furniture, broken flower pot, the soil, and blood—"is not true. I can't imagine Dominic is with these horrible people. I keep hoping the nightmare will stop and I can hold him," she wept. "Will they look after him?"

Scott didn't know what to say. There was the noise of sawing.

"What's Jake doing?" Debra asked.

"Getting some planks ready to barricade the door."

Debra looked puzzled.

"The kidnappers have the keys."

Debra's hand flew to her face. "Of course. How could I forget?"

"Marge Summer invited us to move into their guest wing for now. Shall we?"

"Yes. We are not safe here."

"Debra, my love, I'm so very, very sorry. But for Dominic's sake, we must hurry. Please."

She looked at him with haunted eyes and slowly nodded.

"Can you think of other photos we should take along, apart from the album?" he asked.

"The box of loose pictures. I wanted to send some to Irina."

He released her hands, and she went to get the box.

"Please pack quickly what we need for overnight."

Minutes later, she was back. "I've got everything for the children, I hope. But I didn't pack any of our stuff yet."

He smiled. She always considered their children's needs first, before her own. He felt a near physical pain as he thought about her suffering and headed toward the door.

Jake intercepted him. "I'll board up as soon as you're ready. Got everything?"

"Almost," shouted Debra from the bedroom. She was at the car with a second bag by the time Scott had pulled himself behind the wheel.

"Got a toy for Dominic?" asked Jake.

"What for? asked Scott.

"When he returns."

Debra bolted back into the house and returned with the white teddy bear and its red "I love you" sash.

chapter 28
CALLS OF HOPE

THE AROMAS OF North Indian curry and freshly baked roti wafted out the door to welcome an angry and frustrated Fernando. His domestic servants were experts in divining their employer's quirks and moods. They knew that having his favorite dishes ready could help turn a bad day into a good one. Lunchtime had long passed, and Fernando hadn't had a nibble or drink since early morning. He had not even stopped to wash off the grime and sweat from the construction site. Ravenous as he was, he knew he would enjoy his food even more after a scrub, which he hoped would also ease the tension in his neck. The rush of water always had a calming effect on his nerves.

Rivulets of water trickled from his long, black curls onto his barrel chest and hairy back as Fernando stepped into a pair of clean cotton trousers. He was just starting to dry his hair when the phone rang. He made a dash for it.

"Yes, inspector, thank you for calling."

The inspector general of the police told Fernando that everything possible was being done to find the missing child. "Mr. Singh, will you keep me informed about all developments, regardless of the day and hour?"

"Certainly, sir."

"I'm on holiday right now, but I don't mind being disturbed. No trouble is too much. Just call this number."

Fernando took note.

As soon as Fernando put down the phone, it rang again. The caller was a lady officer from the child protection unit, a department of the South African Police. A radio station in Johannesburg claimed Dominic Warrington had been kidnapped, she said. The same station had given her Mr. Singh's phone number. Would he be so kind and tell her what had transpired so far?

Fernando didn't take long to fill her in.

"We really need help from your government," he said in closing.

"The local police are not up to this, and if the Warringtons are right, this is a crime organized across international borders."

"Let me assure you, Mr. Singh, we are working on this in South Africa."

"That's not enough. We need help here. We are getting platitudes from the local authorities. Our police do not have enough cars, not enough training."

"Surely you understand we are not in a position to interfere in the affairs of another sovereign nation. But if your head of police requests our assistance, we can respond."

Fernando thanked her and dialed the private number the inspector general had just given him. The phone rang for a long time before it was picked up. Fernando related his conversation with the South African Police and got the impression that the inspector general grew increasingly. But he thanked Fernando for the information and said the South African police would be invited to assist in the search for the kidnappers and the child.

Fernando wolfed down his lukewarm curry and headed for NoiseBoys.

chapter 29

ON THE AIRWAVES: MALCOLM
IN THE MINIBUS

THE BUS TERMINAL was always busy, but today the frantic excitement had reached a feverish pitch. Everywhere Malcolm Maziger could see, people were poring over the newly printed posters depicting baby Dominic Warrington. He listened to the excited chatter around him as he took his place in line at the terminal.

A baby kidnapped! What a thought. A reward of 150,000 Kwanzos. Who had ever heard of such a thing? Everybody wanted to lay their hand on a poster.

"Free copy for you?" asked a sweaty vendor who had forgotten about the wares he balanced on a simulated cardboard shelf supported by a string around his neck. His display exhibited biscuits, pictures of the pope, condoms, rat poison, handkerchiefs, batteries, and much more. His grubby hand pushed a poster into Malcom's line of vision.

"No, thanks." Malcolm carried close to a hundred copies of the reward notices in his bag, which he was to take to the nearest border post.

A rusty minibus pulled up sporting a grubby piece of cardboard with "border" scribbled on it. There was the usual scramble for seats. The bus appeared fully loaded when Malcolm entered, but the conductor motioned to three passengers already on a bench to make room for him. He was glad to get a ride at all.

Next to him sat a weather-beaten, grey-haired man and a beautiful young woman. A chattering little girl with exquisitely braided hair sat on her lap. Behind them, four adults plus a few children arranged themselves on each of the four bench seats. The seats were so worn that metal springs poked into Malcolm's backside, scuffing his trousers. Every inch of narrow space between the last bench and the rear door was crammed with purchases from Kasiki town. Blankets, bags of maize, and various bundles of bulky merchandise prevented the back door from clicking shut. Instead, it was tied down with rubber straps, cut from used inner tubes.

There was no space for the money collector to sit, but he managed to force his way back into the van with amazing grace and agility. By exerting considerable muscle power, he closed what was once a sliding door but was now held in place by crude hinges bolted to a thin metal body. Welding joints jutted out like ugly scars.

None had ever seen a coat of paint.

The passengers handed over their fares while the overloaded minibus sputtered past maize patches and huts, thumping Swahili rumba music from oversized speakers. At the approach of the full hour, the music faded out and the news started.

The kidnapping was the first item on the list. The newsreader gave the main story and announced the reward of 150,000 Kwanzos for information leading to the safe return of the white baby, Dominic Warrington. The old man next to Malcolm briefly took hold of the babbling child's wrists and laid his finger over his lips. "Shhh."

"We have with us in the studio Debra Warrington, the adoptive mother of the kidnapped baby. Mrs. Warrington, what is your message to our listeners?"

"We are frantic and heartbroken. We don't know if Dominic is alive or dead. Please let us or the nearest police station know anything that might help getting Dominic back quickly. Even if it's just to let us know he is OK. We need to see him, hear him, hold him."

The newsreader thanked her, announced several phone numbers to call with information, and continued with other news.

The driver reduced the radio volume. Nobody spoke. Malcolm guessed several passengers tried to calculate how long they would need to work to earn 150,000 Kwanzos. He guessed that none of the passengers had ever held that amount of money in their hands.

Then, as if in response to some signal, they seemed to talk all at once. Some bemoaned the violence, some expressed sympathy for the child, some for the mother, and some wondered about possible motives for the kidnapping. Everybody fervently hoped to catch a glimpse of that white child and pick up the reward.

The old man sighed and shook his head. "Terrible thing. Terrible."

"The Warringtons are good people," Malcolm said. "I know them."

"This country has changed so much. They say we have freedom, but what kind freedom? Freedom to snatch little children, steal, murder. Now even white people. Nobody is safe."

chapter 30
MORE TO THE HUNT—CLIVE

LIVE ARCHER WAS tinkering with the steering mechanism of his 1300 Datsun pickup. It was a well-travelled, modest vehicle, but it was his very own. His father, a bank manager, didn't believe in giving out pocket money. Clive had paid for his beloved truck with several years' worth of savings and money earned slaving at fisheries and pig farms during school breaks.

Clive had just begun greasing the front axle when his Dad rushed out of the house yelling something about the Warringtons' baby.

"The boy's been kidnapped!" said Rodney Archer. "I'm off to find out more." He jumped into his car and sped off.

Clive packed up most of his father's tools and rushed to the house. He grabbed a six-pack of Coke, some biltong, and a loaf of bread from the pantry. From the garage he retrieved a ten-liter water container, which he threw into his truck. On the way to Kasiki, he collected his African friends Augusto and Dumisani. Both sold curios and were streetwise.

At NoiseBoys they saw lots of vehicles parked, among them those of Clive's parents. Scores of people from all races and professional backgrounds milled about. Some were genuinely concerned about the missing child, some just plain nosey.

Clive learned the Warringtons were holed up in the office with a police sketch artist to compile identikits of the kidnappers. Jake Vermeulen, whom Clive had met several times before, appealed for volunteers to form a search party. Clive and his friends said they were as good as ready to go and just needed to fill up their water container.

"Got a cell phone?"

Neither Clive nor his friends owned one. They shook their heads. Jake handed Clive a brand-new mobile phone. "Go easy on it. It's on loan from the distributor and must remain salable. I hope you'll have reception. If not, go on higher ground. Start at the back of Kasiki mountain and work your way toward the border. Find out if Dominic was taken that way. Spread the news. If you meet suspicious characters, don't confront them. Let me know what's happening, and we'll decide how to respond. Are you OK for a day or so, if need be?"

"We have nothing to cook with, but we will be OK for a day."

"Good. If you are not back by noon tomorrow, we'll send a search party after you." Pointing at the Datsun, Jake cautioned, "Your sardine tin might get stuck."

"It might. But I have a rescue committee with me," Clive replied, grinning at Augusto and Dumisani. Clive's mother, Darlene, handed them a stack of posters to take along and a box of thumbtacks.

"Now, you'll be careful, will you?"

"Yes, ma'am," Dumisani smiled.

chapter 31

MALCOLM AT THE BORDER

THE BORDER WAS as congested as ever, smelling of diesel fumes and rotting mangoes. He swatted at green flies buzzing around his face. Malcolm knew it wouldn't be much longer before the border would close for the night. He noticed the drivers of large trucks carrying industrial goods nervously hoping to be cleared before the boom came down, and the drivers of small commercial vehicles haggling with customs inspectors about wares and charges. Bus passengers urinated on the roadside one minute and bought dough-nuts from grubby, underaged hawkers the next. Fashionably dressed youth in glitzy jewelry traded foreign currency, which was illegal but made a few quick bucks.

Malcolm observed this situation while he took his place in the line of patient humanity waiting for exit stamps from one country and the entry stamps for the next. He noticed two officials stepping outside their office. Malcolm left his place in the line and drew them aside.

"Good afternoon, gentlemen. How do you do?" Greetings were always appropriate, no matter how urgent the business.

"Fine, thanks for asking."

"I brought something for you," Malcolm said, and handed them the reward notices.

The officers' eyes popped. Had he presented them with an offi-cial endorsement that he was a delegate from an important group of people, he couldn't have obtained more eagerness to please.

Malcolm cut the formalities short and quizzed them about any suspicious movements.

"We know about the kidnapping and have kept on the lookout, but it's unlikely the child and his kidnappers slipped through our post this afternoon."

"I'll hang about until after the border closes. I'll talk to you again in the morning. Thank you so much for your assistance. Please pass these out." Malcolm pointed to the notices in the officials' hands.

"It's the least we can do. We'll hand these out right away."

The notices were in the hands of other officials, vendors, and bus drivers within three minutes. In the absence of movie theaters and even national television channels, the kidnapping of a white child was a major event. Malcolm saw people huddling in groups the moment they laid hands on the posters. Genuine concern mingled with sensationalism, producing a potent substance that begged to be shared communally.

chapter 32
KIDNAPPERS AT THE BORDER

WHILE THE KID was asleep, it would have been easy to throw a blanket over him and smuggle him across the border. But shortly before they reached the border post, he woke up and howled again. Rufus parked out of sight, tight against the wall of a storage shed. He didn't take a chance on anybody seeing the white kid. Any window facing the road he covered with the blanket or a shirt.

Rufus backtracked on foot to a bottle store. He bought a Fanta for the kid and six bottles of beer for himself and Baldy.

While Baldy tried to pacify the kid with the fizzy drink and biscuits, Rufus hiked the five hundred or so meters to the border post. What he discovered made his skin crawl. Boys were handing out leaflets with a slightly younger picture of the kid on it. He gave a coin to a street urchin in exchange for a full-sized poster. A reward of 150,000 Kwanzos was promised for information on baby Dominic. Rufus cursed and ducked out of sight. Nothing was going according to plan. Castledyn would be beside himself. But no matter his threat, Rufus would not risk getting caught smuggling the kid across this border post. No way.

Instead of returning along the main road, he cautiously weaved his way through side streets to where the truck was parked. He went through a mental list of potential contacts to call on. Nearly all of them were connected with Silver. Rufus shivered at the memory of that man's chilling farewell.

What was meant to be a quick and simple job was turning into a nightmare.

The kid had been sick again, and Rufus felt like leaving him to the loving care of Baldy and walking away from it all. But that would never work. Baldy would learn of the reward offer. He would spill the beans within mere hours, and that would not do. No sir. Certainly not.

chapter 33

DEBRA AT NOISEBOYS

JAKE VERMEULEN'S WORKSHOP was teeming with people who brought phones, maps, a white board, and flip charts. Scott, Jake, and Christopher discussed possible escape routes and strategies to prevent the kidnappers from using them.

Debra sat in the office overhearing the discussion in detached silence. Through the window she watched her friend Darlene Archer arrange refreshments on tables and give updates to scores of people dropping by for tidbits of news.

An old Indian lady dressed in a dark red sari shuffled toward her, extending a gift basket laden with steaming eats. Debra caught a whiff of cardamom and cloves.

"A little something for the men searching for that poor baby," she said. "And some money. They will need petrol and things." She pressed a number of folded notes into Darlene's hands.

"Thank you so very, very much, Mrs. Pratesh. This is very considerate. Would you allow me to write you a receipt for the money?"

"Not necessary," she said.

"Oh, I need to record this anyway. Let me write you one out."

As far as Debra knew, nobody had asked Darlene to do any of the things she just did so quietly and efficiently.

Debra felt like she was on a roller coaster, not knowing if she wanted to scream or to curl up and hide. She knew she ought to be grateful that so many people came forward to help. She could not stop thinking about Dominic. Where was he? What were they doing to him? How bad was his head injured after his horrendous crash into the flowerpot? Question followed question, and answers eluded her. The ache in her heart threatened to suffocate her, and she silently prayed for relief.

She watched their friend Jake for a while and smiled for the first time in hours. Jake was a favorite with the children, but he had never mastered the finer art of diplomacy. Today he strutted around sourcing radios, phones, back-up batteries, and torches. He dispatched various teams in search of information, instructing them to look for anything suspicious in the markets, townships, and pubs. Debra knew he was a deep thinker but never would have guessed that he had such potential for strategic planning and crisis management. Jake wasted few words on formalities but effectively debriefed men coming in from search parties or roadblocks. He sifted through their feedback and passed to Scott and Christopher any morsel of information that held the vaguest hope of usefulness. He barked orders, challenged people's qualifications for certain jobs, and offended several people within the first few hours.

Debra continued to brood. An insurance manager decried the escalating crime and the ineffectiveness of the police. A businessman from her church agreed and demanded draconian measures. The pitch rose to alarming levels. Everybody seemed to have strong opinions on what should be done. Scott intervened.

"Hold it…Hold it. While there is cause for alarm and upset, let's get one thing straight. With every passing hour the dangers to Dominic's life and health increase. Can we please focus on one common goal—finding Dominic." He made eye contact with the men in the room and everyone became quiet.

Debra couldn't believe how her husband could be so collected in the midst of such turmoil.

Scott continued, "Let me fill you in. Dominic is our second adopted child. We suspect that Dominic's biological father, Anthony Castledyn, is somehow involved in this. The mother made arrangements for us to receive Dominic at his birth, but Castledyn fought the adoption in the South African courts, which denied his claims. Our lawyer and the South African police are unable to locate him. He might be here in this very country trying to smuggle Dominic out. Official border posts have been alerted, but we know there are places where a high clearance vehicle could slip across the border. Jake sent men in four by four vehicles to the crossing points within six hours travelling range. As I speak, volunteers are hiking the mountains searching for leads. Their reports are coming in. I've heard of villagers digging a ditch across one road, making it impossible for a vehicle to sneak past."

He pointed to a stack of posters with a big photo of Dominic. It was taken at his first birthday, Debra remembered with another stab of pain. The word *Kidnapped* was written in large letters at the top, and several phone numbers appeared at the bottom, together with a promise of 150,000 Kwanzos for information about Dominic's whereabouts. Scott continued, "Drivers and conductors of local buses are distributing these along their routes."

Debra jumped off her seat at the first ring of the phone. Scott reached for it.

Everybody's attention was riveted on his facial expressions, which displayed yet more dashed hopes for a useful lead. Debra paced like a caged tigress. She was grateful for the many people eager to make themselves useful, but it would be dark shortly. Where was Dominic? Was he hungry, thirsty, sick? Would they give him water polluted with cholera or amoebas? Since the day he was born, he had never been out of earshot from her. He would be frantic by now.

She had to do something or go mad. She slipped out of the room and asked Darlene for two cups of water. She downed one and placed the other in front of Scott, who gratefully accepted it. Both understood he couldn't risk another bladder infection, a constant concern for paraplegics.

Jake interjected. "Chris is trying to get at least one policeman to join us at each roadblock. Anybody available to help, please follow me."

The room emptied. Debra felt Scott's gaze on her.

"It's getting dark, my love," he said. "You should be with Jasmina. She needs you."

"I want to be here when they find Dominic."

"I know, my love. I'll phone you the moment there is a breakthrough, OK? Get some rest."

"How much longer will it take?" Her swollen breasts hurt. She looked at her watch. It was 5:25 in the afternoon. "It has been ten hours since I nursed him."

"I'm sorry, Debra. I wish I knew. I don't know why it happened."

Debra nodded and hung her head. She knew that on the inside Scott hurt too. She embraced him and kissed his cheek.

Christopher got up and offered to drop Debra at the Summers's. "Is that OK, Scott?"

"Thanks, Chris."

chapter 34
A FRESH LEAD

YOUNG AND DANGEROUS, that's what these kids are," said Rodney Archer of his son Clive.

"I wouldn't worry about him," said Jake. "He brought his friends, and they want to help. They may stumble across something none of us would have thought of."

"Jake!" Was that Darlene Archer shouting at him? He had never known her to raise her voice. "Jake, Dominic might be just up the road!"

"What are you saying, woman?" He saw her standing next to an African teenager in jeans and tennis shoes.

"This young lady here says there is a maroon BMW parked at the curb outside the Golden Sentinel this very moment with a black guy and white child that looks like the child on the poster."

The Golden Sentinel, a four-star hotel, was a mere three hundred meters from their position. Jake yelled some instructions, and a dozen people dashed to their cars. Another five just ran toward the hotel. Three minutes later, Rodney's silver Audi station wagon screeched to a stop alongside the BMW 3 Series.

The driver, an African in a suit, must have seen people approaching. He jumped into the car, gunned the engine, and pulled away. Without reflection, Rodney leaped from his car toward the moving BMW. "Stop!"

He was ignored. Billy, in his VW minibus, gave chase, but the VW's horsepower was no match for the BMW. Rodney returned to his car and followed, overtaking Billy in time to see the BMW in the distance turning toward Kasiki township. Once inside the maze of the township road's turns and twists, he lost his prey. Just outside of Silver's driveway he turned his Audi around. He recognized the familiar vehicles of his friends, who also stopped and turned around.

The drivers talked but couldn't agree on the exact license number of the BMW. Had they missed Dominic so narrowly? Was there a white child in the car? If not, what could have prompted its flight? While most drivers combed the neighborhood, Rodney returned to NoiseBoys to report the failed pursuit.

chapter 35

MEDIA MADNESS

WITH EACH HOUR, Irina Coetze grew more frantic with worry about Dominic. She paced, she prayed, she pleaded. After nearly two years of drama to ensure her son was in a loving and secure home, she couldn't believe he had now been kidnapped. Against her forehead she pressed a folded towel, which her mother soaked in ice water every so often. She had been plagued by headaches for many months, and pills alone didn't really do it for her.

Untouched on the bedside table sat a plate with sandwiches and a glass of guava juice.

"You haven't eaten anything since breakfast," her mother lamented. "At least have some of your favorite juice before the next call."

Both were desperate for news about Dominic, but most callers were concerned friends, police officers, or reporters. The media caused her the most headaches. Experience had taught her to say as little as possible to them. She was always wondering how her answers might be twisted and turned against her. She must not say anything inflammatory against Anthony either, she reminded herself. He and his lawyer wouldn't miss a chance to drag her back into court or give the sensational press another chance to plaster her name and face on their front pages. But she was tired of always being guarded. Adrenalin had kept her alert, but for how much longer could she hang in there?

Her mother picked up the ringing phone and listened but a moment.

"Irina, it's SABC news. They want to know how you feel about Dominic being abducted in Mondawa."

Irina sat up and flung the towel against the wall.

"How do they think I feel?"

"Hello...Yes, I'm Irina Coetze, and Dominic Warrington is my son...Tell you what. These people can do what they like to me, but they must leave my baby alone. I will kill them with my bare hands, I swear. I am so angry."

Chapter 36

KIDNAPPERS MYSTIFIED

RUFUS WAS HYPERVENTILATING with stress. He was starting to suspect Castledyn of double-crossing him. It was as if every move he made was countered. Maybe an evil spell had been cast over this venture.

It started on their way to the Warringtons' house when that large truck blocked the road, forcing them to hide the car much farther away from the house than they had planned. Then that Warrington woman came after them, screaming and shouting. Instead of going straight to the car, they had to go over the back fence and through the forest. Then those old ladies spotted them. Rotten luck! They hiked through the bush as both the humidity and temperatures soared. Thistles slowed their progress, and vines trapped their feet. They nearly missed the entrance to the hidden gate of Silver's compound. Just when they thought they were safe, the Silvers chased them away. Castledyn's rotten woman had flown the coop, and the police had a welcome committee at the airport to present him a set of handcuffs for his troubles. Then the debacle at the border and their latest attempt to courier the kid with a so-called businessman got him nearly busted again. This was ridiculous.

He didn't like to admit it, but his options were running out. He would have to appeal to Silver.

chapter 37
CLIVE BLOCKS A BORDER-CROSSING POINT

THE MAJORITY OF roads in southern Africa are simply rutted dirt tracks. In the rainy season, heavy vehicles often churn the softer patches into muddy quagmires. Clive nevertheless enjoyed the challenging driving conditions in the rural areas while his friends told jokes. They laughed so much they had to work hard on presenting a serious face whenever they happened upon people. However, they did stop and tell the story.

An hour into their journey, they were covered in mud from pushing the truck through several muddy patches. In the fading daylight, they stopped where most times of the year a mere rivulet crossed the road. It was now a good three meters wide.

"I don't think we'll make it," Clive said.

"Why not? It's just water."

"I wish I had four-wheel drive."

"We'll have to push," Dumisani said.

"Yeah, but with little clearance I could easily flood the carburetor. Then we've had it. Maybe we should turn around."

"What? We are close to the border and the Ngoli trading center. We can't just turn around now," said Dumisani.

"How far is Ngoli?"

"Not far."

"Agh, you people always say, 'Not far.' Tell me in distance or in how long it takes to walk there."

"Maybe the same as from the airport to the bus station. But remember, people go to sleep with the chickens."

"Let me check how deep the water is," Clive said.

He got out, folded up his trouser legs, took off his shoes, and waded into the water. The water surface came halfway up his calves, but the bottom seemed firm. There was not much current. Clive studied the layout of the land. Trees hemmed him in to the right. To his left, big roots and rocks could easily tear up his chassis. There was really only one small section where he would stand a chance to squeeze across. What the heck. *This is as good a chance to test this truck as I'll get in quite a while*, he thought. "OK, let's go."

"Shall we push?" They were already taking off their shoes, as well as their trousers. *Smart move*, Clive thought. *Why didn't I think of doing this?* His trouser legs dragged water.

"Put your shoes back on, for better traction. Then go and stand over there in the stream, ready to support this beauty," Clive advised. "Get out of the way of the truck at first, but be close at hand as soon as it struggles. I can't afford to stop. A stationary vehicle in this muck will be a heck of a job to get going again. I'll come in fast. Get ready for a free shower."

The guys took off their T-shirts and placed them together with their trousers behind the bench. Clive cautiously reversed ten meters up the hill. He changed gear, took a deep breath, let out the clutch, and then pressed the accelerator. The truck shot forward. Shortly before the water's edge, Clive shifted into second gear to keep the revolutions low. He got exactly to the middle of the stream, and there the little Datsun stopped dead before the other guys could get to it. No amount of pushing and heaving advanced the truck even a inch. Clive wanted to curse but caught himself in time. He groaned instead and stepped from the truck into the water.

"Sorry," Dumisani said.

Clive looked around. No quick solution came to mind. They would need at least a high-clearance four-wheel-drive vehicle, ideally one fitted with a winch, to pull them out.

Clive took the cell phone Jake had given him from the cubby hole and stared at it. "No reception," he grunted. Wonderful. "Now what?" he asked.

"We walk," Augusto said.

"How far to the next settlement?"

"Not much farther."

"You Africans! Be specific. I don't want to hike ten kilometers."

"Maybe two."

They held little hope of finding a truck with a winch that could pull them out, but they could at least further their mission by spreading the news, distributing the posters and hopefully finding a generous soul to make them a cup of tea.

"OK, let's move it. Dumisani, can you take the posters? I'll bring some food. Augusto, grab a container with water, please. I don't want us to catch cholera drinking village water. Oh, and hand me that box of thumbtacks from the cubbyhole, please." He looked around. The moon hadn't quite decided to cooperate yet. "Actually, we may as well start right here." He returned to the truck and switched on the headlamps. Together they stuck posters on the trunks of the nearest trees.

"Who lives out here?" Clive asked.

"People," Dumisani informed him. "There are villages everywhere—even if you don't see them. There could be a thousand people in this district. Believe it or not, their trading center even has a tavern."

"Now, that cheers me up. Let's go."

It started to rain while they marched for about forty minutes through a forest. Then the clouds parted and the moon shone through. Suddenly they stopped and gawked. On a stick in the middle of a clearing hung the very same reward notice with Dominic's picture they held in their hands. How it had gotten there in such a short time was beyond their comprehension.

"This is the border," Dumisani declared.

"You're kidding," said Clive.

"Sure. Look." He pointed at a rusty sign nearby, indicating the national boundary.

"I would never have guessed it. And where is that trading center with the pub?" asked Clive.

Dumisani pointed. "About two more kilometers. Wanna go?"

"May as well. We can't exactly go home to bed just yet."

chapter 38

A CHILD'S PREDICTION

DEBRA FOUND THE two girls playing with dolls in the living room. Both were happy to see her.

"I'm sorry, Michaela, that you didn't really get your party."

"Auntie, we had lots of cakes and ice cream. Mommy said Jasmina can sleep over." Her eyes shone. Jasmina was her best friend.

"Yes, and I see you've already bathed and are wearing your jammies. Teeth brushed?"

Both girls nodded.

"Ready for bed? Go on ahead. I'll be right there and tuck you in."

The girls giggled as Debra entered their room. Debra envied their lightheartedness. But, as if she sensed her mother's heavy heart, Jasmina became serious, sat up, and asked, "Are the bad men going to hell because they stole Dominic?"

I wish! Sorry, God, Debra thought as she sat at the edge of the bed. She answered carefully, "All people do unless they are sorry and ask Jesus for forgiveness." Both girls looked at her. "Girls, let's hold hands and pray for Dominic to come back to us soon."

Debra led them in a simple prayer for Dominic, for comfort in his loneliness, and for protection. All three said amen, then Michaela looked up to Debra and said, "Don't worry, Aunty Debra. He'll be back after three days."

Three days? Please, God. Not that long! "Oh?"

Michaela nodded.

"Thank you, Michaela. Now, sleep well, both of you." Debra tucked them in and kissed their foreheads. "You are terrific girls. I'm proud of you."

Jasmina smiled and rolled onto her sleeping side. Debra switched off the light and went out, leaving the door ajar.

chapter 39

THE ROADBLOCK

A T AROUND SEVEN in the evening, an hour after nightfall, Billy Sommer and Aanish Patel helped set up an improvised roadblock. Somebody had brought three empty forty-four-liter metal drums. Aanish dragged in several big rocks. It didn't look pretty, but it served the purpose. They stopped about thirty cars over the next three hours or so. Billy went over most of those with a fine-toothed comb, not taking any chances.

Around midnight a car raced toward them as if attempting to blast through, with lights on full beam. The driver changed his mind at the last minute and came to a screeching halt with less than inches to spare between his front fender and the drums. He obviously didn't want to ruin the posh car, a maroon BMW. Billy immediately suspected it might be the car that had eluded them earlier that day.

He walked up to the driver and his passenger, who were getting out of the car.

"In a hurry?" he said in his American accent.

"None of your business."

"Maybe not. Did you know a child was kidnapped today?" Billy asked while scanning the interior for any sign of Dominic.

"So they say. What do you want?"

"We'd like to look in your trunk. Please open up."

"Want to look in what?"

"Your trunk. I mean *boot.*"

"Now what? Since when do we have American and Indian policemen?" the driver growled.

Billy asked the attending police constable to please repeat the request to open the luggage compartment. He did, and this time the driver released the boot. It contained a set of foreign car registration plates.

"What's this?" Billy barked. "You change plates like socks— depending on your mood, or what? Show me your ID and driver's license."

No response, apart from a glare.

"Constable, kindly request inspection of those d—ah, documents."

The driver didn't respond. Billy moved to the windscreen, looking for the license disc, but didn't find it.

"You are driving a stolen car. Admit it."

Stony silence.

"Who owns this car?" Billy shouted.

"I do," claimed the driver.

"Where is your license disc?"

"I lost it recently," he said.

"You are a liar," Billy shouted and grabbed him by the collar. The African pushed him right back. Billy was about to strike the driver when the policeman intervened.

"This is better handled at the station, I suggest."

Billy nodded. His two adversaries retreated to their BMW. The policeman was following Billy toward his VW minibus when Aanish cautioned, "Better accompany these men in their car."

It made sense. Billy steered the policeman into the backseat of the BMW and dropped in beside him.

chapter 40

CONFRONTATION AT THE POLICE STATION

A T THE POLICE station, Billy was amazed to find the officer on duty being very friendly with the driver, calling him "brother" and treating him like an old friend. He couldn't follow the conversation, which had switched into Swahili. Billy fumed and left them chatting inside. From the car park, he called Scott.

"We may have one, if not two, of the kidnappers. Can you come to the police station right away?"

"I will be there shortly."

About seven minutes later, Patel's Toyota Prado pulled in, bringing Scott.

"These guys are bad apples," Billy told Scott through the Prado's open window.

"I'm sure the car is stolen. They are inside chatting like old friends with the duty officer."

Patel left his Prado and inspected the unlocked BMW. He opened the door and noticed a cell phone between the seats. He retrieved it and quickly scanned its memory. He came and stood next to Billy, yet addressed Scott.

"Of the last ten calls they made, one was to Silver, three to known gangsters, and four to Asian businessmen with dicey reputations. The other two I don't know."

Scott contemplated. "I don't want them to recognize me," he said.

"You remain in the car," Billy said. "Aanish, when they come out, ask them to walk toward the Prado. Turn on the headlights. That way, Scott, you will remain unseen."

Just then the two suspects walked toward their BMW, which was parked before the Toyota Prado. Scott found the switch and turned on the headlights. They squinted and turned away from the glaring light. Billy opened Scott's door. The cabin light went on, exposing Scott. Billy cursed and slammed the door, feeling very stupid.

"Don't worry, Billy. These are not the guys who took Dominic."

chapter 41

CONVOY

J AKE VERMEULEN WAS in charge of the roadblocks. Some reports disturbed him. That hot-headed preacher, for example, could be downright abusive. And the motorists—some were understanding and accommodating; others were not.

The volunteers, though motivated by a noble cause, could not legitimately search anybody. The presence of the few policemen was useful and gave their daring venture a veneer of respectability. Christopher White had already picked up bad vibes from official quarters.

Jake's radio crackled to life. It was Fernando, hiding in the hills, his night vision binoculars trained on Silver's compound.

"There's strange activity here. Trucks being loaded, cargo unidentified. There are lots of men around. They might be leaving soon."

"Thanks. We will prepare a welcome committee," Jake answered. "Tell us when they are leaving."

"Will do. Over and out."

Jake looked at his watch. It was 12:54 and raining. He pulled his raincoat tighter. Jake saw the look of loss in Scott's demeanor over Dominic, compounded with disappointment that a paraplegic really had no place at a roadblock after midnight.

Fernando came online again.

"A convoy of four semi-covered trucks is preparing to leave. Some carry armed men. Over."

"Good work. We'll meet them at the junction."

Silver's compound was hemmed in by the mountain. Many footpaths led out of the township, but there was only one road for all the cars, buses, or trucks. It connected with the main road at the very junction that had a roadblock in place, manned by five volunteers and three policemen. Jake was sure the net was closing on Silver.

With the help of the volunteers, Jake reinforced the roadblock. It wouldn't hold out long against four trucks but would at least slow and damage them if they tried to burst through. He fervently hoped there would be no show of force.

Thirty minutes later there was still no word. He couldn't contain his anxiety anymore and spoke into his radio:

"Fernando, do you read me?"

"Loud and clear."

"Did the trucks turn back?"

"Nope. Should be with you by now."

"What kind of trucks are we talking about?"

"More substantial than light pickup trucks. More like five-tonners."

"How can four trucks just disappear?" Jake shrieked. "Hold it. I hear something. Trucks are coming. I see lights, but—but from the wrong direction. From town."

Two Bedford trucks rolled up. The volunteers jumped into position and flagged the trucks down. They came to a grinding stop. Jake shone his torch into the bed of the first truck and whistled. On wooden benches along three sides of the bed hunched seven or eight men. They glared at him. Most of them were armed but wore civilian clothes. It was the same in the other truck. Jake shone his torch into the truck cabins. A police constable walked up to the driver's window and exchanged a few stiff sentences with the driver before telling Jake, "Let this truck through."

"What?"

"Let them through. We are no match for these guys."

Jake gave the word and the volunteers rolled two drums aside. The trucks pulled away.

Jake contacted Scott and briefed him on what had transpired. "These were no friendly neighbors out hunting rabbits. They had enough firepower to cut us to shreds. If they had Dominic on board, they would either not have approached the roadblock or forced their way through."

"What about the other two trucks, Jake?"

"They disappeared into thin air."

"Wait a minute. I must have misunderstood. You said..."

"No, you didn't misunderstand. I have no clue how they could have averted the roadblock and then have appeared, minus two, from the wrong direction. Let me check with Fernando. Hold the line please, Scott."

"Fernando. Fernando? Expect two trucks. Watch carefully for anything they might be off-loading. Did you read that?"

"Affirmative."

"After that, will you please make contact?"

"Will do. Over and out."

"Scott, sorry."

"That's fine. But I sure would like an explanation of how four trucks can avoid a roadblock on the only road leading out of Kasiki township."

chapter 42

TEARS AND PRAYERS

DEBRA'S MIND WAS buzzing like a fly trapped in a closed jam jar. Her swollen breasts ached and wetness seeped through the fabric of her T-shirt.

I must make sure I can still feed him when they find him.

She showered and wrapped herself in a big towel, brushed her teeth and hair, and debated about what to put on. While Scott had begged her to rest, she wanted to be ready to hit the road at a moment's notice and collect Dominic. How could she even consider sleeping when her baby was injured, hungry, and miserable? Would they mistreat him, leave him alone in the bush? Was he safe from snakes, scorpions, and malaria mosquitoes? There were recent reports that leopards had taken livestock.

Oh, God, look after my baby, please. Bring him back.

She took out a clean set of clothes and got half dressed. Then she turned off the lights and sat up in the Summers's guest bed. The curtains allowed the outside security lights to shimmer through, casting the room into a post-dawn glow. Dogs barked in the distance, while Debra expressed milk into a tumbler.

Why are you doing this to us, God? We dedicated Dominic to you. We meant it. Are you testing us? Dominic is your responsibility. Why did you allow what happened today? Don't you care?

Tears paused on her chin before uniting with others and falling in big drops on her chest. *Every drop is a prayer for Dominic. Keep him safe, Lord. Keep him safe.*

She put the tumbler aside, completed her wardrobe, and pulled up the covers. Sheer exhaustion induced slumber. She dreamed of violence and danger.

chapter 43

SPECIAL INVESTIGATOR

ANISH PATEL LEARNED that the special investigator of police, Detective Luwimpi, had returned to the capital city in a chauffeur-driven government car and could possibly be found in a seedy hotel bar.

It was close to midnight when Aanish and Billy got there. The air was thick with cigarette smoke and the sickly sweet smell of unwashed bodies. Several men danced and smooched with much younger, scantily dressed women. Aanish and Billy asked about Detective Luwimpi.

"Over there," said the barman with a nod toward a corner where a fat, middle-aged man in rumpled, civilian clothes sprawled in a stuffed armchair.

"At least he is not with a woman," said Aanish from a safe distance. They walked up to him.

"Detective Luwimpi?"

The man nodded in acknowledgement. Even in the dim lights, his sweaty face and drunken demeanor were apparent.

"I am Billy Summer, and this is Aanish Patel. We hear you returned to Kasiki today to help search for Dominic Warrington."

"The police will help you. We will help you find the baby. Don't worry," he slurred.

"Detective, the infant has been gone for twelve hours. We understand your problems with transport and communication. Citizens like Mr. Summer, I, and many others are offering the use of our cars, radios, and phones. Let's work together," Aanish said.

"Work together, yes." He belched. "Sorry."

"But also work together with the police in other countries. They can and want to help. They need your invitation," Aanish continued.

"This is a police matter. No interference. We have a good police force. We will help you." His face clouded over. After a moment he contracted the muscles around his eyes and shook his head slightly, as if he was making a conscious effort to usher the facts from the hearing center into the board room where decisions were made.

"Help us how?" Billy almost shouted. "The baby might have left the country by now. The search at Silver's house was no real search. That place is packed with stolen goods. An eyewitness saw a white child being carried into Silver's compound. Why are you so afraid of that crook?"

Luwimpi slid even lower in his chair but didn't answer. Billy shrugged in disgust toward the door.

"Let's move. We're wasting our time."

Only Patel, ever polite and worried about maintaining the peace, bothered to bid farewell.

chapter 44

THE BUNDLE IN THE NIGHT

A S ONE OF Silver's men, Umar was accustomed to receiving strange orders. Moving weapons, ammunition, communication equipment, food, and water was neither normal nor uncommon. Big Boss was in the vilest of moods, and Umar had witnessed a man being beaten to a bloody pulp because Silver just fancied being entertained this way. Everyone around him was on high alert.

Men and supplies had been coming into Silver's compound since late afternoon, mostly in passenger cars. Silver got highly agitated when he heard of a roadblock halfway between the market and Kasiki town. He sent men in several cars to check it out and report back to him.

Instead of waiting another day for the remainder of the supplies to arrive, Silver decided to move the stuff right away, two Bedford trucks full.

"Put on these fatigues and boots!"

Umar did, and saluted. The drivers of the two supply trucks did likewise. Two additional trucks started up, and the men in civilian clothes clambered on. One truck went before the one that transported the supplies and had Umar in the passenger seat. The other tailed the second supply truck in order to protect it. As usual, only the captains knew what was going on. They saw themselves like a kind of army.

They pulled out to the main road, then followed a narrow path along the market toward the outer perimeter of the township. The big trucks tore branches off trees, filling the night air with the intoxicating smells of African blossoms but also damaging the roofs of homes and flattening fenced-in vegetable gardens. They crossed a stream. Umar knew the area well but would have never believed it possible that a truck, let alone four trucks, could go where they went—and during the night at that!

After many twists and turns, they stopped in the middle of nowhere. His fellow travelers went into position around the supply trucks as if they were defending them against an alien army. Umar was confused and tried not to show it. He climbed from the truck and crouched next to it. It started to drizzle.

A guy appeared as if from outer space. Nobody troubled him. He walked straight up to Umar and, without so much as a word, handed him a bundle of what looked like damp clothes. But it wasn't.

"Get back into the truck!"

Umar did as told by the captain. He arranged the bundle on his lap, groped, and found a face—the face of a small, sleeping child.

They were on the move again and linked up with the old, now disused road that led to a former border post. But only the supply trucks, the two drivers, and Umar—and the bundle with the face—headed in that direction. The other two trucks, empty but for the men, turned right toward Kasiki town.

They bounced down a track where shackled African slaves destined for Arab markets once marched toward the coast. Nearing the former border post, they found the dirt road flooded. That was expected this time of the year. But they were stupefied to find the only safe crossing for a Bedford thoroughly blocked by a Datsun bakkie, which was obviously not designed for such conditions. Sitting next to Umar, the truck driver cursed. Umar assumed he didn't like the idea of having to clear the obstacle in the dark and in the rain, but he was wrong. The driver pointed to some white, rectangular surfaces against the tree trunks on the opposite banks. The driver maneuvered the truck in position to shine full beams on them. They read:

KIDNAPPED

There was a picture below the big letters. Umar lit a match and held it over the bundle. The face was different but not much. There was no question in his mind that it belonged to the child on the poster. Information had deliberately been kept from the men working for Silver, but now a great many things made sense to Umar: The flurry of nervous activity at Silver's house, the roadblock, the unorthodox route of travelling, the dramatic pickup of the child.

"Check how long these bloody papers have been there."

Umar put the bundle on the seat, hopped off the truck, and waded through the cool water. He didn't need a degree to establish the basic facts. Within minutes he was back in the truck. "Not long. Papers are clean, not even soaked through yet. No corrosion on the metal tacks. Couple of hours at the most."

The bundle moved and whined. Driver and passenger looked at each other, thinking about a way to ignore the child, who was now howling.

"We can't cross without moving the bakkie," said the driver. "A rescue truck team might be on its way already and suspect we have the child. If we lead them to our destination, we are dead meat, no matter which country we try to hide in."

"Is there a different way?"

"There always is. But the rain is getting worse. The dampness gets into the electronics we're hauling and messes them up. We'll abort. Tell the other driver."

chapter 45

A NEW PLAN

HEN BILLY AND Aanish arrived back at NoiseBoys shortly
before 1:00 a.m., their report did little to cheer the weary
group of volunteers. After the encounter with Silver's thugs
at the roadblock, they were keenly aware that they lacked the muscle
to enforce a wide-scale search. Scott felt the need to discuss options, so
he gathered the volunteers in the NoiseBoys front office. Empty coffee
cups, sticky sugar spoons, and wrappers from hamburgers and sweets
littered the brightly lit room. As they gathered, the men all seemed to
talk simultaneously. Scott had to shout to be heard above the din.

"The police are clearly afraid and appear to be under orders to play
things down. The special investigator is drunk and probably scared to
death. But let's go back to the topic of the reward versus ransom."

"So far, the kidnappers have not demanded anything other than
what they already got—Dominic. A decision had to be made, and we
made it collectively based on the amount of money pledged."

Scott's statement reignited the debate about rampant crime and
ineffective police.

"A big payout will start a new problem—child-snatching for reward. I
advise against paying any money," said Roberto Azolin, a local farmer.

"One hundred and fifty thousand Kwanzos have been offered. It's a
promise and must stand. We can't go back on our word."

"I hear that the president's advisor, Mr. Raffik, wants us to raise the
reward to two million. Is it true?"

"Well, in dollar terms, two million could possibly be raised if we
all dug very deeply into savings and investments. It's a human life we
are talking about, is it not so?"

"It will not remain just one life. From now on, each of our lives could
be on offer to the highest bidder. Do we know what we are doing?"

"Wasn't this the kidnappers' plan all along, in cahoots with high-
placed officials, to get rich quick? No child, woman, or man will be
safe any longer. Where are the police in all this? They are all idiots,
Silver's mafia."

"Remember the Lindbergh case. They paid a reward of $50,000. That didn't save the child's life."

People murmured and Scott continued. "In this climate of insecurity and fear, we need an incentive for people to come forward quickly with information. That just might make the difference between life and death for Dominic." He looked around and ascertained he had the men's agreement.

"What about your embassy, Scott? Did you contact them?" asked Aanish Patel.

"Yes, I informed the South African Embassy. I got through to somebody telling me proper channels must be followed—whatever that may mean."

"Bureaucracy!" said Christopher White, exasperated. "We should have a representative of your government sitting here in this very room with us now."

"Hey," said Rodney Archer, "this is a crisis. How many South Africans do we have in here right now?" He counted five hands. "OK. Come over here to the phone. This time we accept no excuses. We need to speak with the South African ambassador now. Shove his beauty sleep. This calls for his intervention. Dominic is South African, and so are his parents. Scott, you still maintain that Anthony Castledyn, a South African, is behind the kidnapping?"

"Yes."

"So I say we force this ambassador, or his representative, or whatever his title is, to get beyond his colonial guilt complex. We demand that our embassy gets involved." A murmur of support went up, and Scott handed him the phone and a slip of paper with the numbers.

chapter 46

WAKE-UP CALL

A SHRILL NOISE STABBED his befuddled consciousness. He couldn't breathe. A voice. A familiar woman's voice. It was Debra, saying to hold on. She dove for the ringing phone on Scott's side table and was sprawled out on top of him. He squinted and found himself in a strange bedroom. He barely made out the time on the bedside clock. It was 5:30 a.m. He'd slept less than an hour. His head throbbed, and he felt groggy. As Debra rolled off him, he noticed her facial expression changing from eager expectation to disappointment.

"South African News Agency, asking for a briefing," she said and handed him the receiver.

So it was true. Dominic's disappearance was a painful reality. He felt unprepared to receive an important international call. He gritted his teeth and managed to give a short summary of the developments since Saturday afternoon. No, there was no word from the kidnappers, no notice for ransom, no leads. Yes, he still believed Anthony Castledyn, the biological father in South Africa, was involved. No, the local police were not on top of things. Any help from South Africa would be appreciated.

"Take this to President Nelson Mandela. Ask him to put pressure on the government of Mondawa to ask for help from South Africa."

Scott hung up the phone and closed his eyes, bone weary. He wanted Dominic to be safe and back home *now*. How could this have happened? He should have taken more precautions. He should have checked that the watchman had locked the gate when he left. He was lazy, naïve, reckless. Again. Stupid.

Debra rolled on her arm and looked into his face.

"That was bold," she said.

"What?"

"To appeal to Mandela."

Scott didn't know how to answer. He'd just followed an impulse.

"I don't know what else to do, Debs. We failed to stop them. Who knows where they are now?"

Debra knew he was speaking about the kidnappers and Dominic. "Just as well, you alerted the media to the South African connection. I would never have thought of appealing to Mandela, though." She reached across and caressed his face. He needed a shave.

"How are you, my love?" Scott asked.

"What can I say? I want Dominic back. My mind keeps replaying that moment when his head smashed against that stupid flower pot. I should never have put it there. He might be badly hurt from that. You think they might abuse and mistreat him?"

"If Castledyn wants him, he wants him alive and well."

"Sure," Debra answered, "but when the heat is up like this, the kidnappers might panic and...do something stupid. If I just hadn't let go of him. I was so afraid of tearing him apart."

Scott reached out and stroked her cheek ever so lightly and said with more confidence than he felt, "Debra, don't torment yourself. God gave Dominic to us. He won't let us down now. We did the best we could for both our children. And now we'll again do the best we can to find Dominic quickly. The Lord is watching over us and over Dominic. Just think of how many people are out there searching, helping, praying."

Debra stroked Scott's arm. "Do you know what Michaela said yesterday?"

"No, what?"

"She said he will be back in three days."

Scott pulled back. "Three days? Can you imagine two more days like yesterday? No way."

"Didn't you read the story of Jonah to the children, just before it happened?"

"Yes."

"Jonah was in the belly of the fish for three days and three nights."

"Yes?"

"That's an awfully long time, trapped like that," she reminded him, "not knowing he would get out alive."

Scott pulled Debra close and kissed the top of her head. "Maybe this is a sign. We must face the fact that we may not find him today.

But I don't know how we will get through even one more day of this anguish."

Debra hugged him tightly. Scott was tempted to linger but remembered something.

"Debs, get ready. The police are sending the sketch artist first thing this morning with the drafted identikit. We must be at NoiseBoys by 6:30."

She nodded but didn't release him yet. The next moment she threw back the sheets, stepped out of bed, and said, "I'll run your bath and check on Jasmina."

Scott nodded and struggled into his chair.

chapter 47

NO GOLD FROM SILVER

RUFUS FELT LIKE a hunted animal. Everywhere he went there were reward posters. And not just posters showing the kid. Now there were new posters with sketches of him and Baldy. It seemed like any hope of getting the contract money was fading by the minute. He was desperate for a stiff drink but couldn't risk going to a store or bar to buy one. Instead, he holed up in the shack near the airport and fell asleep. Next thing he knew, Rufus felt the muzzle of a gun at his head.

"Get up. Nice and quiet, buddy."

Two huge guys dressed in sweaty old fatigues blindfolded him and pushed him into a waiting car. After a ride of less than thirty minutes they took him to what smelled like a dank, smelly dungeon. They took off his blindfold. Rufus blinked against the single light bulb and recognized Silver with some of his heavies. On the floor cowered Baldy, all beat up and bleeding from a split lip and some grazes.

"So we meet again," Silver said. "I could have done without the pleasure of ever laying eyes on you again. You give me nothing but trouble."

One of the heavies punched him in the stomach.

"I mean you no trouble, boss," Rufus said.

"You bring me a stolen child, the police, half the townspeople, angry calls from the president, and the inspector of police. What do you mean, no trouble?"

Another punch landed in Rufus's stomach and brought him to his knees. Before he could get up, a boot kicked the feet from under him, throwing him flat on his face.

"Easy," Silver cautioned. "I need him coherent for a little while."

Somebody grabbed him by his afro and yanked him down on a chair. Silver sat opposite him smoking a cigarette. "Tell me how I find myself mixed up in all of this."

Rufus didn't feel like explaining anything. He just wanted to be sick and curl up in a ball.

About six other mean-looking characters glared at him.

"Cat got your mouth? Make him talk."

The guard who had punched him earlier got into position to attack Rufus afresh. Rufus spread out his hand in a futile attempt to protect himself. He shrank against the back of the chair.

"Not necessary."

"Speak up or you're dead," Silver said.

"Castledyn told us to bring the child to your house. There would be nappies and food and our job would be done. You would give us the money he owes us."

Silver laughed. "He said so, did he? You are naïve, boy, very naïve. But tell me, how did you hook up with him?"

"A friend introduced us. Told us his child had been taken from him by so-called missionaries and taken to our home country, Mondawa. He was desperate and would pay anything to get him back."

"Ah, and you thought he was good for the money?"

"He's a white man. Yes."

Silver sniggered.

"He wore good clothes, talked, and argued like one of those posh, rich people you see on TV."

"Yes, I believed him." He didn't say he also was impressed by that hot chick who followed him like his shadow.

"No. You were greedy."

"He was on television, man. Speaking about his kid. I wanted to help him."

"You're lying, man."

Silver put out his cigarette and lit another one. Rufus was feeling very cold. He had heard so many bad stories about this madman. He would not tell him that he had been living in South Africa as an illegal immigrant, in trouble with the law as well as with some low-lifes, and was anxious for a break.

"What were the arrangements?"

"Just snatch the child. His woman would take the child to South Africa, either by car or by plane. But she didn't come through."

"I know that. How much did he pay you?"

"We haggled over the price for a while, then settled for a cash amount that seemed fair, plus a secondhand car. He came through with the car but only 10 percent of the agreed price. The rest upon delivery to Silver in your country,' Castledyn told us. I pressed him for the cost of the transfer up front. He didn't like that and said he would feed us to the Greek mafia and do the job himself."

"So he owes you?"

"Big time. Somehow I doubt he will ever pay me, now that he's got the kid."

Silver gave him a cold stare. "He doesn't."

Rufus was stupefied. "But the kid is well across the border by now."

Silver signaled with his head. The guard yanked Rufus up and dragged him into a dark corner. Another guard shone a torch on a familiar-looking bundle. It was the kid, fast asleep.

Rufus didn't understand. The guard dragged him back to face Silver.

"Complications," Silver said with ice in his voice. "And I don't like complications. You two take the kid and forget you ever saw my face. Is that clear?"

Rufus nodded, well aware that the slightest slip of the tongue could cost his life. He and Baldy were blindfolded and frogmarched to a truck. Rufus heard the muffled whimpers of a child. Before long the crying bundle landed in Rufus's lap, and they started to move.

When the truck finally stopped, the guards pulled open the door. "Get out! All of you!"

Rufus scooped up the baby and joined Baldy outside. He had no clue where they were. There were no buildings anywhere in sight, just trees and bush. The truck took off.

"How can that jerk just dump us?" groaned Baldy.

"Be glad we're alive."

The Warrington boy started whimpering again. Rufus handed the bundle to his buddy. "Keep him quiet, Baldy. Let's start walking before the sun comes up. Stupid me for ever taking this stinking job!" Rufus surveyed the area and checked for an indication of the early morning sun.

"We can't risk being seen with him. Now let's get moving."

chapter 48

COMMUNITY EFFORT

AT NoiseBoys Scott and Debra encountered a barrage of questions from local news reporters. By the time they finished, Jake was pacing, eager to get started with a morning briefing.

At his signal, about twenty men and women filed into the office. They were fatigued, unkempt, and grateful for sandwiches and cups of fresh coffee. At 7:10 a.m., Scott called the meeting to order and prayed.

"Debra and I want to thank you all for your support yesterday and last night. Some of you have not been to bed for over twenty-four hours. We know you, too, are disappointed we haven't found Dominic yet. We believe he is still in this country and will be returned to us soon, and alive."

Some men mumbled agreement, others wanted to debate. Scott plowed on. "We need small units to tackle a number of issues. Each team meets as often as necessary. Team leaders, please consult with me regarding major decisions." He wheeled himself to the whiteboard, which, on Jake's initiative, was lowered so Scott could use it. In bold letters he wrote, "Operation Jonah." Underneath he scribbled a bulleted list of concerns: roadblocks, accounts, government/police, publicity/media, intelligence, catering. "Let me hear your suggestions as to potential team leaders."

Lively consultation ensued, and soon each listed item had the name of a volunteer next to it. Jake's name was next to "roadblocks." Rodney, a bank manager, was nominated for accounts. Darlene would oversee catering. Christopher White seemed the obvious choice to handle government relations and intelligence. Publicity stayed open for the time being. They grappled with the complexity of coordinating a nationwide hunt and came away with a clearer picture of what needed to be done by whom and when. This eased the sense of frustration and helplessness they had faced the previous night.

"We can't right all that is wrong," Christopher White said. "But let's make our presence felt. When it comes to injustice and evil, we no longer 'accept things as they are.' Let's go after these gangsters until we find Dominic!"

chapter 49

GOOD NEIGHBOR

DARLENE ARCHER PARKED her car on the empty street and waited. The shops were still closed, but in a couple of hours, this section of town would be like an anthill, teeming with pedestrians, vendors, and motorists competing for every square inch of space along the major commercial road. Muslims and Hindus owned the majority of shops, petrol stations, and clinics in town. Most of the Asian shopkeepers were Africa-born. Now, shortly before seven on a Sunday morning, the place smelled clean, even though the stillness felt uncanny. Daytime guards, some of them in smart uniforms, relieved the night watchmen. They greeted each other like friends and brothers.

Darlene was sure the kidnapping featured prominently in their stories, adding substance and variety to their entrenched gossip patterns. Darlene guessed that several of the men were at this very moment also discussing her and her car, yet she felt no cause for alarm. Kassim Muammar would appear any moment after his morning prayers at the mosque.

She noticed the security men getting up smartly. The next moment, Kassim parked next to her in his Mercedes Benz. He was clad in a long robe and a skull cap. He greeted her and handed over a set of keys to one of his staff to unlock the shop.

"Any news on the child?"

"None, I'm afraid," said Darlene.

"Terrible business. Terrible."

"Thank you so very much for opening your shop this morning."

"Don't mention it. Glad to help. You brought a list?"

"Yes. Ten heavy-duty cooking pots, thirty flashlights with a double set of batteries, thirty boxes of thumbtacks, fifty rolls of Scotch tape. Here is my card with our church's address. Can you make the bill out to the church?"

"No bill. This is my contribution. It's cruel to steal a child. Cruel. Let's pray to God he is found quickly. Return the pots once the men who are searching the bush are done with them." Kassim called out quantities and articles. The men gathered all the goods and piled them on the counter. He then turned to the watchmen and addressed them in a Creole mixture of local and foreign languages. The men responded in a similar tongue.

"Sorry. They also have not been able to gain any helpful information on the kidnapping. I will lock up and go to pray in the mosque now for the child to return safely."

"Thank you. You've been very kind. Greet your wife."

"I certainly will, Mrs. Archer."

chapter 50

DEVIL ON THE RUN

N LESS THAN twenty-four hours, news of the kidnapping spread far
beyond Mondawa. Through the initiative of Theresa van Rooyen,
Fernando, Billy, the Archers, other missionaries, and friends and
relatives of the Warringtons, updates were flashed to the African news
media. Other updates were phoned, faxed, and e-mailed worldwide,
encouraging people to pray.

As Christians in the Kasiki region met for Sunday morning services,
there was a new focus in prayer. Over a hundred churches from all
kinds of theological persuasions united in praying for the child. They
prayed for Dominic Warrington to be returned to his parents with
speed and in good health.

In rural Mondawa churchgoers celebrated Sunday services in
scattered grass-thatched huts. Members of these congregations were
typically subsistence farmers. When the harvest was good, they had
enough to eat. In times of drought or flood, as now, they often went
hungry. Even in good years, cash was always in short supply.

The only chairs available to congregants were concrete slabs with
no back support. On a raised platform at the front of the church sat
the elders, men in ill-matching suits, on wooden chairs made with
basic tools. Dusty plastic flowers stood in a rusty tin on the altar.
They contrasted sharply with the resonance of African voices singing
praises to God with enthusiasm and harmony as only Africans can.
The only instruments used were handmade drums and tambourines,
but the sound was gloriously harmonious, joyful, and full of vigor and
conviction.

After the singing at one rural church, the pastor hushed the congregation and told them about Dominic and the need for urgent prayer.
And pray they did—simultaneously. Some at the top of their voices.
Some crying, some kneeling, some pleading, some commanding the
powers of the devil to crumble. It was all truly noisy and truly from
the heart. From church to church across Mondawa, such prayers
rocked the heavens.

At the same time, at the southern tip of the African continent, about four hundred people, mostly white and some of color, came to the services of the church where Irina was a member. The pastor told of the kidnapping of Irina's biological child from his adoptive parents up in Africa and her planned trip to be with them. He asked Irina and the elders to come forward. Irina faced the congregation, and about ten men and women stood in a circle around her, some of them slightly touching her shoulders. The pastor placed his hands on Irina's head and prayed for her.

"May the heavenly Father give you peace, wisdom, and travelling mercies. May He protect the child and restore him to his adoptive parents quickly. Amen."

As people prepared to return to their seats, a lady in the congregation got to her feet. She said she felt she had a word from God for Irina and asked permission to share it. Permission was granted, and she was ushered toward the microphone, next to where Irina and the elders were standing.

"I see the baby being held in somebody's arms," she said, smiling at Irina. "I can't see the face of the person holding Dominic. But angels surround that person and the child. The Lord says to you, Irina, that He watches over Dominic. The child is safe."

Irina, with tears in her eyes, squeezed the lady's hand and thanked her quietly. She felt encouraged and humbled, loved and supported by her church family. She thanked the pastor and the congregation and returned to her seat.

After church, several people assured Irina they would continue to pray for her and Dominic until he was safely returned.

chapter 51

A FRIEND IN HIGH PLACES

AHMED RAFFIK WAS bothered by something in his throat. He stopped his black government-issued Mercedes Benz at the petrol shop to look for cough lozenges. He was pleased to find the manager, Vina Naidoo, at the till. Her brother, Aanish Patel, had gone to high school with Ahmed. After the country's independence, non-African kids such as Aanish, Vina, and Ahmed were no longer allowed in government schools. They attended private schools that pooled students from the community of aid agencies, missionaries, expatriate contract workers, and Asian traders.

Ahmed came from an Indian Muslim background. During school hours, Indian students tended to stick together like glue. Out-of-school socializing was restricted to even tighter Muslim or Hindu cliques. This sometimes led to mild forms of gangsterism. Ahmed managed to navigate through this social maze and developed friendships outside his cultural group. This skill no doubt enabled him to maneuver his way into high office.

Vina Naidoo asked him politely if he was well and then demanded to know what the president was doing to assist in the search for Dominic.

"That's a delicate question, Vina."

"How so? The whole town is in an uproar. Our men are confronting criminals head-on, while the police couldn't care less. Crooks are parading in the streets, intimidating innocent people. They are behind bars one day, let go the next.

"The kidnapping affair stinks, and you, being the president's right-hand man, ought to know that."

"Whoa. Slow down. Tell me what you've heard so far."

Vina blurted out what she knew, which made her feel a little better.

"I agree, this is most disconcerting. His Excellency must be informed." Raffik took her hand and squeezed it gently. "Can I ask you a very big favor, please?"

Her long, dark curls bobbed about her head as she gave a guarded nod.

"I am sorry for inconveniencing you," he said.

"Don't think of it. There are lots of people out on the streets, sacrificing their Sunday. If that child can just be found quickly, that's all we want."

"That's very kind. You are very sensitive and caring. Your husband is lucky to have you."

She smiled. "What do you suggest I do?"

"Write everything down. What you know, what you have heard, what Warrington and his friends are doing, and what they expect will happen."

"And then?"

"Address the letter to me, Ahmed Raffik, Public Relations Officer, Kurumba Palace. Drop it off at the gate of the palace. I will hear the minute it arrives."

"Shall I sign it?"

"Of course. I'm planning to show it to His Excellency. It's useless without your name and signature. If you are not sure of something, say so. Say, 'It is rumored...' or 'I understand that....'"

"OK, Mr. Raffik. I'll try."

He laughed. "Since when am I 'Mr. Raffik' to you? I'm still Ahmed, right?"

"Right."

At the door he turned once more, smiled, and waved to her. The moment he was gone she phoned her brother.

chapter 52
WARRINGTONS AT NOISEBOYS

GIVE ME A break, man. Of course we don't intentionally withhold information from you. It's been a madhouse from the moment of the kidnapping. We haven't had time to twiddle our thumbs or plot how long to hold out on you with the news. Grow up!"

Scott shook the phone and scowled. In spite of all the pressure around her, Debra couldn't help but smile. Some people could be so childish, wanting to be the first ones called with any updates. She craned her neck out of their cubicle and noticed more reporters with cameras coming up the ramp. She quickly retreated into their hiding place, pausing for a moment to feel her swollen breasts. Dominic must be screaming to be fed. *Yes. Give them a hard time. Tell them to take you to your mommy.*

She peeped out again and saw a woman securing "wanted" posters to the inner workshop walls, the artist's sketches of the kidnappers. Not bad. Darlene Archer had gotten thousands of copies made and added them to the stacks of posters volunteers handed out.

Everybody around Debra seemed busy. *Can't I do something useful for a change?* The thought of this search going on for days staggered her. *It's one thing to find volunteers on a Saturday and Sunday, but if we don't find Dominic today, who will help tomorrow, when everybody is expected back at work?* The pencil she'd been playing with broke. She snapped out of her thoughts and looked at the vandalized pencil with surprise.

Jake looked in, saw Scott on the phone, and disappeared again. She knew he would have interrupted if anything were breaking. Her chair was uncomfortable. Every muscle in her neck seemed knotted. She fidgeted and was pleased Scott finally put down the receiver. He had a concerned look on his face as he looked at her.

"You OK?"

Stupid question. "Guess so. You?"

"Yeah. Some people can be so self-centered. I'm afraid I don't have time for this right now."

"Scott, isn't there anything I can do to help find Dominic?"

He considered her for a moment, shifting his weight in his chair. He was about to say something when Valerie Vermeulen, Jake's wife, stuck her head in the doorway.

"Can I come in?"

"Sure, if you don't mind being cramped. No chair, I'm afraid," Scott said.

"I don't." She embraced Debra and leaned against a corner.

"How are you holding up?" She glanced from Debra to Scott and back to Debra.

"Pretty low," Debra said. "Every time the phone rings or somebody runs in I am on tenterhooks—most of the time, actually."

"I know you want to hear me say that everything will be OK. But is that realistic? Are you bracing yourselves for bad news?"

"What are you saying, Valerie?" Scott demanded.

"All I'm saying is that I really hope Dominic is OK and everything will turn out fine. But you must face the facts." She had the Warringtons's undivided attention. "The chances for a small child surviving a kidnapping diminish drastically every twelve hours. Amateurs at kidnapping are dangerous."

"What are you trying to tell us, Valerie?"

"I don't want to frighten you. But remember the Lindbergh case?"

"What about it?" Debra asked, remembering that it ended badly.

"His mother kissed him goodnight. That's the last time she saw the baby alive. They paid a hefty ransom, but the child was already dead."

"No, I will not accept it," Debra cried.

"You must stay calm."

"Stay calm? Are you crazy? You're telling me my child might be dead and in the same breath expect me to stay calm?" Debra was shouting now. She didn't know if she was hurt, angry, tired, or all three. She definitely had had enough of Valerie's bull dust.

Scott chimed in. "We don't need to hear stuff like that right now. I will not entertain it!"

"By all means, hope for the best," Valerie continued, "but brace yourselves for the worst. Let go. Don't hold on so tight. Why don't you tell Castledyn he can have Dominic? It might save his life."

"You aren't serious?" Scott gasped.

"I am. Contact him. He should know where the child is and can lead you to him. You do believe Dominic is still in the country, don't you?"

Scott remembered a claim Castledyn reputedly had made that afternoon, saying he had a Recce team on standby. Scott closed his eyes and spoke deliberately. "I wonder if Castledyn might attempt to paint us as being incompetent to look after Dominic and just let him be kidnapped. He would love to come and find Dominic." He looked at Debra and said, "I cannot and will not trust him."

"Why don't you tell her about Ishmael?" Debra suggested.

"Remember Ishmael in the Bible? Both the child and his mother Hagar were dying of thirst in the dessert. She put the whimpering child under a shrub to die and walked away. God heard the boy crying. An angel told Hagar not to be afraid and return to the child. God would make him into a great nation. Then God opened her eyes and she saw water." Scott took off his broken glasses and wiped them. "He's the same God today and will provide a solution."

Rodney appeared. "There are more reporters, some with cameras. They want to see you, Scott. When can you meet with them?"

"Give them a cup of tea. I'll be there just now."

Rodney gave the thumbs-up sign and disappeared.

Debra said, "There have been signs, we believe from God. We are calling this initiative to find Dominic 'Operation Jonah.' Three days. By tomorrow, I expect Dominic back."

Valerie shrugged her shoulders.

"Pray for us," Scott begged. "Pray for our boy and those holding him captive. Please."

She nodded.

"And thank you, Valerie, for your concern and especially for letting Jake work with us. I don't know what we would do without him."

"You're welcome. See ya."

chapter 53
A TIP-OFF

IR-CONDITIONING WOULD HAVE been most welcome in this tropical heat. NoiseBoys, like so many other businesses, struggled under the double yoke of heavy taxes and soaring theft. Air-conditioners belonged in the category of luxuries. Scott's polo shirt clung to his body, revealing dark patches of sweat on the back and front.

Reporters hung at his heels for information like stray dogs scampering for scraps. While talking to reporters was inconvenient, Scott knew he needed to accommodate them. Dominic's life hung in the balance, and the scales tipped easily.

The moment Scott and Debra concluded their interview, Christopher White ushered the reporters out of the door.

"News," he said in a low voice, making sure that the reporters were well out of earshot. "A guy in South Africa claims to know where they hold Dominic. Says he was previously offered money by Castledyn to hand Dominic to him, dead or alive. Now listen to this. He says he was to take the child over the nearby mountain to a specific house where he would find food and nappies for the child."

"This description fits Kasiki mountain and Silver's house," Debra said.

"But how can a guy who is thousands of kilometers away know that?" asked Scott. "He may not be credible."

"Possibly not, but let's not dismiss it outright. Honestly, what do you make of it, Scott?"

"Muluka confided that the police have arrested Silver several times already. Every time a higher ranking officer requested the files, and shortly afterwards he walked." Scott rested his head in his hands, elbows against the desk, thinking. They were missing something. There must be more information available about Silver, not just the wild stories about his magical powers. "Let's ask Malcolm. He's returned from the border. He lives close to Silver and is a pretty keen observer. Chris, find out all he knows about Silver and his household."

"Will do."

As Christopher White got up to leave, the phone next to Scott rang again. Scott ignored it for a moment. "Let's not pursue the information from South Africa just yet."

Christopher nodded, and Scott answered the phone while simultaneously filing away the information he had just received, ready to be recalled as soon as new input might tell him where this nugget of intelligence fit into the larger picture.

Later that day Malcolm informed Scott and Debra that Silver's wife was the sister of the inspector general.

"A case of blood being thicker than water," Scott said. "Is there no end to the obstacles?"

chapter 54

THE NEXT MOVE

W HAT WILL HAPPEN come Monday morning?" Debra asked. "This franchise must open for business. Dozens of people earn their keep here."

Scott had to agree. Customer bookings for service, repairs, or modifications needed to be honored. "He might be found any minute. Then the search will be over, and there will be no more need for an operations center like this."

Debra usually admired Scott's easygoing, optimistic nature, but not this time.

"Sure. He might. But he might not. Let's face it. There is no telling how much longer it might take. It might be another day. Jake Vermeulen needs his workshop back. And then what?"

"I don't know, love. The Lord will open something up."

"More than the place, I worry about the men." She looked at her wrist watch. "It's nearly four. Tomorrow morning they are expected at their jobs, and who will search for Dominic after that?"

"Let's do one day at a time, my love. One day at a time." He noticed dark circles under her eyes. "Are you feeling OK about us staying with the Sommers for the time being?"

"Oh, yes. Much better than staying in Kasiki, with the kidnappers holding the keys to our house and car. Scott, as much as possible, let's continue to keep it quiet where we stay. We mustn't put Jasmina at risk."

"Sure. How about you go there now. She mustn't lose her parents, too." He patted her hand and smiled at her. "I'll organize a lift for you."

An hour later the director of The Student, a Christian campus organization, offered the use of their modest, ground-level offices with working phone and fax lines. Scott gratefully accepted.

Scott had once visited The Student, but he couldn't remember much about it. Now he and Christopher White conducted a quick run-through to familiarize themselves with its layout.

"Chris, would the smaller office work for you? I'd rather have the larger one. It's difficult for me to maneuver my chair in such a shoebox."

"Totally fine. You're sure I can use the phone in here right away?"

"Go ahead."

Christopher White immediately settled in and started making calls. He was grateful to escape the hectic activity at NoiseBoys. His interaction with contact people demanded a level of privacy which was not available there. He had been making important calls from his home, but being close to the other volunteers on the ground was critical at this stage.

Little did Scott know how truly well connected Christopher White was.

chapter 55
CHANGING THE ODDS

J AKE VERMEULEN SAW the bewildered look on Scott's face and knew the news he had just received on the phone was not good. "What is it?" he asked, putting down his coffee cup.

Scott just stared at the receiver in his hand and slowly shook his head. Four sets of eyes waited for his answer.

"Some guy says they know where we are. We mustn't think we are safe. It could be a hoax."

"We had better phone the police and let them know," Rodney Archer suggested.

"The police," Scott scoffed. "Can you believe they 'lost' the kidnapper's T-shirt and cap, which I had urged them to take as evidence? It's maddening." His fist hit the table. "Sorry." He took off his broken glasses and tried to clean them. "The police are intimidated. The inspector general has close family ties with Silver and is unwilling to confront him on this. The state president himself is indebted to this crook Silver for favors during the campaign to get into office. My embassy says, 'Mondawans don't kidnap children.' Our volunteers are untrained and do stupid things like manhandling people. Our child has been taken from us by force, and now we get threatening phone calls. The odds are stacked so high against us."

Silence settled on the room. Nobody had ever seen Scott so frustrated and depressed.

"The mobile crime unit," said Jake. "Why are they not helping?"

Scott lifted his hand in a helpless gesture. "What do I know? The MCU reports directly to the president. Chris White hinted that the local authorities are already incensed with us white people running the show."

"So what if they are incensed?" argued Jake. "Good. Let them get upset enough to get up and do something for a change. Scott, phone Chris and tell him about the phone call. Maybe he can use his influence and get the MCU to help."

His radio crackled and, after a brief communication with unseen volunteers, he turned to Roger and Aanish.

"Can you two relieve Fernando and Billy on scouting duty in Kasiki?" Both got up right away. "Just drive around town and especially Kasiki and keep a lookout for anything unusual."

chapter 56

DECISION TIME FOR
THE KIDNAPPERS

BALDY WAS STILL smarting from the beating at the hands of Silver's men. Those guys nearly scared him to death. He told them everything he knew, but they insisted he was holding out on them. Fortunately, Rufus's story was in line with his earlier version. Otherwise, they might have killed him.

Both he and Rufus were dog tired after sneaking around in the dark, trying to find a place to hide.

"There's a shack just up ahead," said Baldy. "We can stop there."

"No. We can't go there with the kid. People might hear him and ask questions."

"The mountain. I see its outline against the horizon. We hide there."

"Do you know how sound travels on a mountain? That cry-baby? We must be where people are used to noisy children. We also need to find food for the kid. With Kasiki mountain over there, Kasiki township is close by. It's less than an hour now until first light. Let's get a move on before the kid wakes up." Rufus pulled the cloth over the child's face.

Baldy started to move out, then stopped in his tracks.

"Hilda," he said.

"Who's that?"

"A girlfriend. She has a daughter about the kid's size and lives alone. She doesn't mix much with people."

"Brilliant idea, except we can't involve any other person. Any one of Silver's men could turn on us. We sure don't need anyone else to know we have the Warrington kid. We just can't risk it."

Baldy considered this for a while. "I'll tell her I have a contagious stomach bug and must rest for twenty-four hours. She will worry about her kid catching it. She sells beans at the market. I'll suggest she go and stay with another young mother for the night."

"Let's go."

chapter 57
SECOND ESCAPE

R ODNEY, AANISH, AND a policeman scanned the surroundings, noting reward and wanted notices on posts, fences, houses, windows, and walls. Hardly any shacks still had lights on. Suddenly Aanish braked and pointed at a dark BMW without number plates.

"This car avoided the search earlier," he said.

He stopped the car at the side of the road and radioed NoiseBoys. "Aanish here. Found the maroon BMW in Kasiki township. Over."

Crackling noises came over the radio, then Jake's voice. "Go and check any details you can find. Over."

"Will do. Over and out." He turned off the radio. "Let's go."

The policeman was the last to emerge from the comfort of the Cruiser. Rodney surveyed the area. Aanish shone a torch into the empty BMW. "Nothing looks out of the ordinary."

"Except there are no registration plates, nor license disc," Rodney said. "This makes identification harder. Give me your torch."

Aanish handed it to him, and Rodney lowered himself under the car, unable to avoid a puddle. In no time his trousers were soaked. A mechanic had shown him once how to release the bonnet catch. He scrambled up and opened the cover over the massive engine, asking Aanish to give him the radio. He shone the torch on the chassis number and spoke into the radio. "Jake, it's a BMW 333i. If I'm not mistaken it's got a 6-cylinder 3.2 litre engine. This is one cool baby, I tell you. Sports suspension, low profile tires—totally out of place in this dump. Date of manufacture, 1986."

Jake had the South African police on the phone and passed the information to them as it came in, instructing Aanish to stand by. Rodney quietly closed the bonnet. He pulled out his handkerchief and wiped at the muck on his trousers. He placed the rear foot mat from the Cruiser on his seat. Everything was eerily quiet until their radio crackled to life again.

"The police in South Africa confirmed that details correspond with their spec list on a car stolen in Pretoria a month ago," Jake said. "Find the guy claiming to own it, but be careful," he cautioned.

Aanish and the policeman knocked at the unlit shack closest to the BMW.

"Who's this?" asked a sleepy young male voice.

"Police," Aanish said, noting the policeman's unease. "We have a few questions."

They heard somebody mumble and move about.

"Ask if that's his car out there," Roger whispered to the policeman.

Two minutes later a wide-eyed kid in his early twenties put his head through a narrow gap in the door, staring at the policeman. The policeman asked about the BMW. The youth said the car belonged to his friend.

"Where is he?"

"At the tavern in town, probably."

"Can you take us to him?"

"Sure. Give me a minute to get dressed."

"A minute, not a second more," Aanish replied and pulled the door closed.

Twenty minutes later they picked up Davie Sulman, a heavy-set forty-year-old, at the tavern and brought him back to the maroon BMW. He didn't fuss at their request to open the boot. Rodney trained his torch light on two sets of number plates lying inside it. One set had local numbers, the other a South African registration.

"Where did you get the car?" Rodney asked.

"Bought it."

"From whom?" asked Aanish

"From a guy called Solomon Banda."

At the mention of that name, the policeman sprang to life, discussing something in a local tongue. After a while Rodney got impatient. He interrupted the discussion and asked the policeman, "Are you taking him to the station?"

The policeman looked shocked. He then contemplated and finally nodded agreement. "Mr. Sulman, we need to take you and the car to the station, please. Got your papers on you?"

Sulman nodded and slid behind the wheel while the policemen stood by passively.

"Hold it," Rodney said. "He shouldn't drive. Officer, why don't you drive?"

"Ah, sorry sir. No license, sir."

"Are you armed?"

"Yes."

"Well, let Sulman drive. But you should sit in the back seat. Make sure you meet us at the station—don't let him get away."

Rodney and Aanish followed in the Land Cruiser. As the BMW approached the roadblock, the brake lights came on. For a moment it seemed that the car would stop, but then the BMW saw a gap and sped past the roadblock. The Cruiser gave chase, but volunteers closed the gap by repositioning one of the drums. By the time the volunteers recognized their friends and opened up, the BMW had disappeared.

Never one to give up easily, Aanish hoped the BMW would head out of town and kept driving. He was rewarded as they spotted the BMW successfully stopped at the next roadblock. As they got closer, they saw the policeman leave the car. The people manning the roadblock, upon seeing the policeman, moved the barrier. The BMW took off again, leaving the policeman behind. Aanish swore.

chapter 58

AN ANGRY PRESIDENT

EQUESTING MRS. NAIDOO to report developments to him in writing was a stroke of genius. Raffik promptly presented her letter to the president. It was only two pages long, but it laid out the main points neatly. The overweight president slouched on his luxury couch and held his hand out for the letter. Raffik gave it to him. A tiny, exquisite East Asian woman massaged his feet.

It was not commonly known that His Excellency, the State President Dr. Abdullah Manukwa, was a miserably slow reader. Raffik was fascinated by the exotic beauty at Manukwa's feet. He wished her hands were ministering to his legs instead of the fat president's, but no way was he going to arouse the president's jealousy. He forced his wandering eyes to move elsewhere.

This palace was full of amazing sights. Since Manukwa had taken over from the previous head of state, millions had been squandered redecorating it with expensive carpets and wall hangings from the Middle East, ornaments from New York, and draperies from South Africa.

Out of the corner of his eye Raffik noticed the president appeared alarmed by what he was reading, maybe even incensed.

"Relax," the imported beauty whispered. "Too tight." She kneaded his arches.

The big man kicked savagely and roared, "Relax? Are you crazy?" He flung the pages across the exquisitely furnished room. They landed in a tray of canapés and a box of Ferrero Rocher chocolates. The girl cringed, bowed low, and scooped up her lotions. She stepped back, eyes downcast.

"Get out."

She vanished.

He struggled to his feet on the thick Persian rug and stared at a huge television set tuned to an American soap opera.

"This is turning into an international incident," he fumed. "The World Bank review is only weeks away and we need their continued goodwill and assistance to fund pressing civic projects."

Ahmed Raffik knew the country was experiencing a major food shortage, and the British ambassador had asked awkward questions about the recently ordered fleet of luxury cars. His Excellency had promised a new Mercedes to each cabinet minister, and now he was under some pressure to deliver.

"This has the power to undermine confidence in our security as a nation." He paced the room. "Those banks have lots of money. But before letting a poor country like Mondawa have any, even as a loan, these Westerners ask for reports, for inspections, for reams of contracts, where they hide ways to manipulate and control us."

Raffik knew there was some truth to all of this. He couldn't set a foot into a half-decent hotel or resort without falling over delegates of one workshop or the other. Politics could be galling business at times.

"Read the rest to me," the president instructed. "Number one."

Raffik walked over to the couch, picked up the offending pages, and reassembled Mrs. Naidoo's letter. Still standing, he cleared his throat and asked, "May I sit?"

The president pointed to a single leather seat, and Raffik sat down and read, "Number one. Sufficient grounds appear to exist for the apprehension of Mr. Silver for questioning. Two eyewitness statements support this. It is understood that he can be legally detained and questioned for up to forty-eight hours."

"The audacity!" The president struggled to his feet. "These are common folk. Meddling," he spat, and traipsed across the room. He opened a generously stocked bar. "Now it's already two witnesses. Previously it was only a child. I bet the second was an adult." He filled a glass with whisky and gulped it down.

"Help yourself," he said as an afterthought.

Raffik shook his head and dismissed the invitation with a wave of his hand. Muslims were not supposed to drink. He was thirsty for water, but the bar wasn't stocked with that commodity. He just wanted to go home. When Manukwa was in one of these moods, there was no telling the outcome of a meeting.

"Fernando Singh and Christopher White complained relentlessly about Silver, the inspector general, and the local police. Now I get a letter from a woman. A woman," he roared, "telling me what to do. Why don't they run the whole country, if they are so clever?" He parked himself on the edge of the couch. "Go on."

"Many local residents have commented on Mr. Silver's activities, but they appear afraid of the man and his bodyguards. Detention of both Mr. Silver and his men would probably encourage local residents to speak more freely. Leaflets offering a reward for any information leading to the whereabouts of the kidnapped infant have been distributed widely, and feedback continues to point toward Mr. Silver. Reports state that Mr. Silver's men stopped and assaulted people distributing these leaflets. This is hardly the action of an innocent man who is not even mentioned in these leaflets." Raffik looked up and saw the big man had reclined in his seat. His eyes were closed.

"May I proceed?"

The president nodded.

"Number two. Request the South African police to arrest the biological father on the grounds of complicity in the kidnapping. After all, in view of his repeated public statements, he is a prime suspect."

"Number three. Request for cooperation between all law enforcement agencies of this country and South Africa."

"Now can you believe this?" the president roared. "She tells us how to run our police and intelligence network! Finished yet?"

"Almost," Raffik said and continued.

"These initial actions would enable your press office to demonstrate to the now-hungry international news media that our government can indeed deal with such a situation. Failure to act *immediately*, however, will only bring unwanted international attention."

"That's a threat. It's like saying, 'Do as we dictate, or we give you bad international press coverage.' It's blackmail. That's what it is." He glared at Raffik. "Do we have options?"

"No, not really. The majority of those helping Warrington hold foreign passports. The story has been on South African TV since yesterday."

"Yesterday? That's when the kidnapping happened. How can that be?"

"I wonder. The point is, the story is out, and every day it seems to attract more attention."

"So, are you also telling me what to do?"

Raffik crossed his expensively clad legs, exposing his designer shoes. "I wouldn't think of it, Your Excellency."

"Liar. Of course you do. Never mind. Let me think this over. Meet me at my office at ten tomorrow." He sat up and stretched out his right hand.

"Help me up."

"Certainly, Your Excellency."

The big man struggled to his feet and left the room without another word. Raffik waited for several minutes before he dared to tip-toe out. It was past midnight.

chapter 59

KIDNAPPERS IN TOWN

At the edge of Kasiki village, less than five hundred meters from two gossiping elders, the kidnappers were holed up with Dominic in a crude shelter normally occupied by a quiet, hard-working girl and her baby. She had managed to find beer, condensed milk, and some biscuits for her sick visitor before slipping away for work, taking along her baby, like she always did. None of the neighbors thought it odd that a baby cried in the shack, nor that the crying went on longer and angrier than usual.

Rufus, unashamedly cashing in on the privileges of seniority, retired to the pitifully thin mattress on the floor nursing two prized bottles of beer. He left Baldy to look after the kid, who was screaming his head off again.

Baldy gouged open the milk tin with his knife and fed the kid some of the sticky yellow content oozing from the massacred container. The boy calmed down instantly, but the respite was short-lived.

"Can't you keep the kid from howling?"

"He's had half the milk, so he shouldn't be hungry. What else can I do?"

"Rock him to sleep. What else? He hasn't had his afternoon nap."

"Are you kidding? Have you looked at this kid lately? He's got poop all over him. I'm having a hard time keeping the flies off my face, especially these green monsters."

"Now you're making sense. Clean him up, man. Clean him up."

Baldy shot him a poisoned look. Rufus rolled over and tried to sleep.

Baldy, devoid of alternatives, sighed and knelt on the floor, inspecting the task at hand before removing the toddler's shorts. He yanked hard at the next layer of cloth but failed to separate them from the child. After careful inspection, he labored, undoing two safety pins with the minimum amount of damage to himself. Finally, he peeled off several layers of cloth. He would have held his nose but he needed both hands to get the soiled and soggy nappy away from the frantic kid. He opened the door and flung the offending parcel out. Draped over a bucket he found a nappy, but it was still wet. He searched some more and found a long, printed cotton cloth that he wound around the baby's dirty bottom.

"Now you better shut up or...Rufus! Listen!"

"Huh?"

Baldy shook him. The whirring sound became a loud throb. A helicopter seemed to approach the hut and hover over it. The place shook, kitchen contents rattled, and gusts of high wind whistled through the rickety shack, whipping up clouds of dust. Both kidnappers held their breath, sweating profusely. After a minute or two, which seemed like half an eternity, the terrifying noise grew fainter. But before their heartbeat could normalize, the helicopter took another sweep before going away.

"Can you believe this?" Rufus said, looking down at Dominic. "I'm nearly having a heart-attack and this kid sleeps through that pounding!"

chapter 60

IRINA ARRIVES IN MONDAWA

WHEN IRINA APPEARED at the arrivals hall of Kasiki airport, she seemed older and thinner than Debra remembered her. Both women were misty-eyed by the time they finished hugging. When they finally turned toward Scott, Irina hugged him, too. It seemed only natural to draw close during such times.

On the way into town, the Warringtons updated Irina on what had been happening. There was still no demand for a ransom, nor any other breakthrough. There were renewed assurances of cooperation from the authorities, but it remained to be seen if those promises were merely lip service or sincere. Unless God intervened, and soon, things looked grim for Dominic.

"Look ahead," Scott told Irina. "See that build-up of traffic from the opposite direction?"

"Yes."

"It's a roadblock, checking cars leaving the city for anything suspicious that might lead us to Dominic."

"Wow."

"There will be many more roadblocks and men tonight."

Scott crawled past a number of people and cars to find a spot to stop where he would cause the least amount of obstruction on an already congested stretch of road.

"It's Scott!" somebody shouted.

It turned out to be Roberto Azolin, a volunteer in the search. He walked up to Scott's window for a quick chat but had no real news. Debra continued Irina's briefing while Scott drove on.

"Since the kidnapping, we've been staying with Billy and Marge Sommer. Will you be OK staying with our friends Valerie and Jake Vermeulen?"

"No problem," replied Irina.

"That's great. They both should be at The Student right now. It's a meeting place for volunteers of Operation Jonah. That's what we're calling this effort to find Dominic."

It was just getting dark as they drove into the packed parking lot. Scott gasped at the size of the crowd. About two hundred people were milling about, amongst them twenty elite soldiers from the mobile crime unit who doubled as presidential guards. All were dressed in battle gear.

A circle of people formed around their car, and eager hands helped retrieve and unfold the wheelchair. Friends, reporters, and strangers fired questions. Scott patiently answered them while he lowered himself into his chair. Debra and Irina headed toward the office, where Darlene Archer and her helpers had set up a soup kitchen that fed over one hundred volunteers.

Debra knew Scott had received several threatening calls earlier in the day but decided against telling Irina about this. Instead, she focused on the good news. "Housewives, missionaries, and other concerned friends meet at Darlene's house in Kasiki every night to pray for Dominic and the search. We've been in touch with Theresa in South Africa at least twice every day. She communicates with other adoptive parents who also pray."

"Wow."

"Yesterday somebody had a vision of Dominic being in a shelter, surrounded by angels."

"That's strange," Irina said. "Somebody in my church had something like a vision while praying and saw Dominic near water."

Debra squeezed Irina's hand. "We never could have mobilized all these people. God did. Jake takes short naps right here, when it's quiet. He hasn't slept in his bed since Saturday morning. And he's not the only one. We must find Dominic soon. It's been three days now and time."

Irina wondered what she meant. Before she could ask for an explanation, a tall, beaming American approached them, and Debra made the introductions.

"My wife, Marge, is expecting you for supper. Scott suggested I drop you ladies there. Is that OK with you, or would you want to first go to your room?"

Irina looked at Debra for guidance.

"If we went straight to Billy and Marge's house, you could say hi and goodnight to Jasmina. She is all excited to meet Aunty Irina."

"Well, let's go then."

chapter 61

ONE FINE MESS

THE HELICOPTER HOVERING over their hideout put the fear of God into the kidnappers. They expected to be busted any minute. Communication with Castledyn had died, Silver was now an enemy rather than an ally, and the kid couldn't be moved and was a huge liability. If it wasn't for the reward money, they might have just made the kid disappear for good. It wouldn't be too hard to get away with. It was time to disentangle themselves from this mess.

Baldy had gone over every inch of space in the small shelter and unearthed a strange assortment of costume items.

"You'll get no marriage proposal, but you'll do," Rufus assured him when Baldy paraded his apparel before him. "Just don't chat up anybody and give away the game with your deep voice."

Dressed like a woman, Baldy snuck out of the shack in the twilight of the passing day. He found his way into the neighborhood of his relatives and waited. A girl, possibly a first-grader, skipped toward him. He attracted her attention and placed a coin and a piece of paper in her hand. She stared at it open-mouthed.

"Abubakar. Know him?" he said, imitating a woman's voice.

She nodded. Of course she knew Abubakar.

"Give it to him right away. Keep the money."

She had been trained to obey adults. Without hesitation, she ran off.

chapter 62

LIKE SHARKS

BILLY BURST INTO the small office where Scott was in a conference with volunteers.

"Scott! I hear somebody claims he knows where Dominic is. True?"

"I don't know yet. Two people offered their help, each for a sizable fee. One's a witch doctor, the other says he's a private investigator."

"And?"

"I don't know. Could be true; could be another red herring."

"Hey," said Billy, "better not tell Debra about it."

"Why not?"

"We mustn't get her hopes up if it turns out to be another hoax."

"We've been married for five years and have never kept secrets from each other. I will not start now."

"You'll phone her with this news?"

"No, I'm going to see her and say goodnight to Jasmina. Tell Chris not to respond to either of these guys. He can call me. Now gentlemen, excuse me, and please help me get out of this matchbox."

Irina got a joyful welcome from Jasmina at Billy and Marge's place. Irina felt like she'd stepped into a whirlwind since arriving in Mondawa.

"I still can't believe how many people are out there looking for Dominic."

"Yeah. Tonight's turnout is the biggest so far. It feels like any moment somebody will turn up with Dominic in their arms."

Suddenly Debra frowned. She jumped up and ran out the door. Irina followed close behind and saw Scott's Land Cruiser turning into the driveway. Debra ran to meet him, expecting to find Dominic in the seat beside him. Why else would Scott be coming home now? But Scott had neither their son, nor good news.

"The girls are in bed already?"

"Yes, but I'm sure they are not yet asleep and will be happy to see you."

Debra followed Scott to the girls' room.

"Daddy, Daddy," Jasmina jumped out of bed. "Did you bring Dominic back to see Aunty Irina?"

"Not yet, Jasmina."

"Will you read us a story?"

"No, my princess, not tonight. But I'll tuck you in and pray with you. OK?"

She was a little disappointed but still happy he was there.

Debra tried to judge what was on Scott's mind. "Why are you not with the other guys, Scott?" she asked the moment he was out of earshot from the girls. "Is there news of Dominic?" She was suddenly very frightened.

"Babe, there is and there isn't."

"What's that supposed to mean?"

They joined Irina and Marge around the table. Scott recalled the latest developments. Debra hung on every word, ready to jump into the Cruiser and travel through the night to get her baby. Scott told her it might be a hoax.

Debra was astounded. "Why would somebody claim to know where Dominic is if it's not true?" She got up and paced the room.

"The money."

"What?"

"To make money. To get the reward."

Debra stood still and asked, "You mean they are just sharks, taking advantage of this crisis?"

"It probably boils down to that."

"I hate them," Debra shrieked. "I hate them all. How can they do this? Have they no heart?" She wailed and pounded her fists against the wall. Irina gently placed her hands on Debra's shoulders.

"It's been three days now," Debra wailed. "It's enough! I can't bear this any longer!"

Irina wrapped her arms around Debra's trembling body and gently turned her face into her own shoulder.

chapter 63
THE DEAL

YOU GET TEN thousand Kwanzos, man, by barely lifting a finger. Have compassion on us. We've worked our butts off for this for weeks—no, months. All we want from you is an hour of your time and sealed lips."

The youth still seemed hesitant. Rufus began to sweat.

"If you want, we will show you the exact location beforehand. Ten thousand Kwanzos. For one hour. What is there to think about?"

"I want to bring my friend along. Ten thousand for him, too."

"No, man. Don't be a fool. The more people who know about our arrangement, the more trouble we'll have. I tell you what—you keep twenty thousand of the reward money. Baldy and I will share the remaining thirty thousand. But don't involve anybody else."

The youth couldn't envision doing something as significant as this on his own. "How can you be sure they will pay?"

"Don't you have eyes, man? The reward notices are everywhere. It's like a promise these white people made to thousands of people. They wouldn't want to upset the locals. They will pay you. Possibly not the same day. But they will. And then you say 'thank you' and pay us commission for finding you such an easy and well-paying job. Yes or no? There are lots of people out there who would do this without blinking."

"OK. I will be here after dark with my friend. Baldy shows us the exact location, then my friend and I will go to the tavern. On the way back we'll hear and find the kid."

"That's my man. Ten thousand for each of you; the rest comes to me and Baldy."

chapter 64
THIRST FOR BLOOD

THE KASIKI SWAMP, less than a kilometer from the edge of the village, buzzed like a biological Grand Central Station at rush hour. The biotope choked on rubbish and other effects of careless civilization, but it still served as a magnificent concert hall. Each night it came alive with complex symphonies of humming, chirping, croaking, and scratching. In the darkness there was movement. Plenty of it. Grass snakes slithered across the uneven ground. Beetles and crickets emerged from the soil. Frogs leaped, rats scurried, and mosquitoes buzzed.

They had all been about their business for a long time, but something was different tonight. A tender human being lay between the reeds, whimpering in pain. About one hundred starving mosquitoes led the first wave of assault, sucking blood from his eyelids, ear lobes, and ankles. The spoils were promising. Hundreds more joined the feast and stung through the tender skin on his face, his arms, and his feet. Ants fed from the dried sugar caked at the child's chin, hands, and throat. The baby kicked and screamed in protest but couldn't shake the invading hordes.

He was weak, and every pore of his tiny body ached. Something stank of rotting waste. He squirmed in dirt—his own and that of the swamp. He wore a red T-shirt and nothing else, making it easy for creepy-crawlies to find raw flesh. The crickets and frogs joined his lament. Worms wriggled around him. Coarse weeds poked him. He was starving, dehydrated, and crying for his mommy in an ever weakening voice.

chapter 66

LETTING THEIR GUARD DOWN

LOSE TO MIDNIGHT, Scott and Debra fell into bed bone weary from worry and fatigue, but sleep eluded them. With so many people mobilized, why had they not found Dominic? Would he ever be found and returned to them? Was their beloved boy dead somewhere? And why, God? Why had He still not answered their prayers? The same anguished thoughts raced through both of their minds. After another bout of turning and tossing, Scott leaned on his elbow and whispered, "What's that sound?"

Debra giggled. "I was wondering when you would notice it. It's the elite soldier from the mobile crime unit, sent here to protect us."

"I don't believe it. Our very own elite soldier guard is snoring outside our bedroom window! I'll tell him to push off."

"Don't. He's here to guard us," Debra cautioned.

"He can join the watchman at the gate."

"That one already has company from this guy's colleague."

Scott fell back into his pillow but couldn't switch off. "How come you know?"

"I brought them tea over an hour ago. It was obviously not strong enough. But if they finished the pot, at least one of them will need bladder relief soon."

Scott groaned. "Let me check in with the men." He grabbed the mobile phone and punched in numbers.

The roadblocks had netted another stolen car, Chris said, but there was no hint of Dominic. The men were all exhausted.

"What do you suggest?" Scott asked.

"Let's remove the roadblocks and hope that a loosening of the screws might encourage the right guys to come forward with information. How are you and Debra?"

"We are trying to sleep. But the MCU guy is snoring so loudly outside our bedroom window, it's ridiculous. "

"Pull him up by his ears."

"It might cause unnecessary commotion. Never mind. At least the children are asleep. Go home, Chris. You've done all you can."

"You really sound depressed, Scott."

"I am. Take care. Talk to you in the morning."

"So long."

chapter 67

STRAYING ON THE WAY

Monday nights were lean nights for the tavern in Asundi village, but they stayed open for Abubakar Nkhomo and his friend William from Kasiki—to a point.

"It's past eleven. Come back tomorrow, if you want," said the big-chested lady who had served their beers.

Abubakar had chosen Asundi because walking home from there would give them a reason to pass the swamp. They had enjoyed spinning ideas of what to do with ten thousand Kwanzos each. They were getting closer to the swamp, and their conversation grew more reflective.

"We are in big trouble if we're caught carrying this child," William said.

"Then we explain that we found the child and are on our way to the police station. And that's the truth."

"I'm not so sure. I've seen ordinary, good people beat a guy accused of pick-pocketing. He cried and begged for his life. That just cheered the mob further, fed their frenzy. We might be beaten to death before we get a chance to say anything. And I don't expect the police to treat us nice, either. They beat up first, ask questions later. We could run into a patrol. Even the president's soldiers are out and about. I wouldn't want to cross them."

They walked on, two troubled souls.

"Somebody can steal the child from us and claim the reward. Even the police might swindle us."

"Tell you what," Abubakar said. "We don't take the child straight to the police. We take it to one of our tribal elders, the village headman, for example. He's a second cousin to my grandfather. We ask him to come to the police with us."

"I don't believe it," Abubakar's friend said. "I was afraid the beers tonight might put you to sleep, but they actually helped you think. What a brilliant idea. I hope nobody has already taken the child."

"Listen. Am I dreaming or do I hear a cry?"

"I hear it, too. I hope it's the child. Let's fetch him."

They took off toward the sound, feeling much better about their mission.

chapter 68

VILLAGE HEADMAN

O DI, ODI," ABUBAKAR said, leaning against the door of the
village headman's home.
No response.

"Odi, odi. Please, it's important. Very important."

"Who is it?"

"Abubakar Nkhomo. We found the child."

"Huh? Hold on, I'm coming."

Shuffling, mumbling, waiting. Footsteps coming closer to the door.
The door opened and the bearded elder squinted at them. The room
behind him was dimly lit.

"Young Nkhomo, you better have a good reason to wake up an old
man at this time of night."

"Sorry, Baba, for calling at such an inconvenient hour. How are
you?"

"Fine, fine. What have you got here?" He peered suspiciously at
them.

"A baby. A white baby. The white baby. And this is my friend
William."

"Let me see...Ah, I can't see in this light. Come in." He stepped
back for them to enter. Abubakar sat down with the child. The baby
urinated. The effect was instant. Abubakar jumped up, holding the
child away from him, but his trousers were already telling the story.

The old man laughed. "I'm listening, young Nkhomo. And you
better not leave out anything."

"We were walking near the swamp, coming from a party in Asundi.
Then we heard a strange noise and went to go see. It sounded like
crying, and sure enough, it was a baby. William and me pulled it up
out of the swamp grass. The mosquitoes, they were eating him alive.
When we saw he was a white child, we thought maybe he's the one
everybody looks for. We held his face up to the poster, and yeah, he
is the one! So we come straight here. I say to William, 'Headman he
knows what to do.'"

"Good, very good." The old man was pleased that his opinion was being sought.

"Will you come to the police with us, please?"

"Surely not in the middle of the night. Very first thing tomorrow morning."

The boys' faces mirrored disappointment. They had paid for their beers with borrowed money, but they could afford to wait a few hours before their loan would haunt them.

"When the first rooster crows, get up and come here. Together we walk to the police station. My wife is sick, but I'll find some water for the child." He got up and disappeared behind a curtain. He returned with a plastic cup and handed it to Abubakar.

"Water. For the child."

Abubakar held the cup to the child's lips. He seemed disinterested at first. Abubakar tipped the cup and a little water passed the child's lips and trickled into the opening of his sticky, red T-shirt. The child reached toward the cup and Abubakar repeated his performance. This time the child drank greedily. The old man disappeared for a second time. When he returned he carried a piece of local cloth. It was old and faded. He shuffled over to a rag on which a dog slept. He kicked the dog and chased him away. Then he threw the cloth over the rag. "Put the child down here," he said. "It's warm."

Abubakar did as ordered.

"Now, let's all try to get some sleep. You too, little white man. Stop whining. You will be home soon."

chapter 69

THE DARKNESS BEFORE THE DAWN

SCOTT EASED HIS aching and utterly exhausted body into the hot, soapy water. He thought a bath might help refresh him after another restless night. While the warmth soothed his body, it did nothing to relieve the deep ache in his soul. *Three nights now and still no word of Dominic. Surely we have suffered enough! God, don't you care?* He slipped below the surface and waited until the last possible moment before coming up, gasping for air. Mindful of other people being close by, he fought the temptation to cry out in anguish and anger. Instead, he reached for the shampoo bottle and unscrewed it.

Every time he tried to quiet his troubled mind, new thoughts assaulted him.

They had been through so much with Dominic, even without the kidnapping. He still could almost taste the pain he experienced over the adoption being rescinded. He remembered their appeal and feverish anticipation of the court's judgment.

Through that long adoption battle, he and Debra had checked and rechecked their hearts for any underlying motives of selfishness. Should they be content to raise Jasmina as a single child? What was God's plan for them as a family and for Dominic? He smeared shampoo on top of his head and made some half-hearted gestures to work it into a lather. *O, Lord, You helped us then. Are you abandoning us now? Have we lost Dominic for good? O, Lord, I don't accept that we will lose him by such violent means. That's not Your way. That's not Your character. Help!* An agonized groan escaped from the pit of Scott's stomach, while the tub swallowed his tears. He dipped under the suds again, half wishing to remain there instead of facing the darkest day of his life. He had to pull himself together.

Scott broke through the surface of the water. His gasp for air merged with another groan of utter misery.

Billy burst into the guest wing.

"Scott!"

Debra's voice came from the bedroom. "He's in the bath."

Billy pounded on the bathroom door. He didn't wait for a response. "Scott! They found him!"

Silence.

"Scott, hurry! They found him!"

Then he heard Scott's broken voice faintly behind the closed door. "Found who?"

"Dominic, of course. That's who we've been looking for, isn't it?"

Again, Scott didn't respond right away, but Debra flew toward the bathroom door and tore it open, shoving Billy aside.

Scott sat covered in suds, but both he and Debra blurted out the same question almost simultaneously: "Where is he?"

"At the police station," said Billy from the doorway. Debra stood next to Scott's wheelchair, beaming broadly.

"It will take me at least ten minutes to get ready," said Scott, shampoo running into his eyes. "Go with Billy, Debs. I'll follow as quickly as I can."

"You'll get out OK on your own?" asked Billy.

"Yeah. I've had plenty of practice. Go!"

Billy raced after Debra, who made straight for Billy's VW Combi in the driveway. Again, she wore no shoes.

chapter 70

UNIFICATION

Though it was just seven in the morning, masses of spectators were converging on the Kasiki police station like floodwaters in rainy season. He recognized a number of friends, but many faces belonged to villagers he'd never met before. Billy nudged his VW Combi through the crowd while Debra sat ready to bolt for the station at any moment.

"OK, now go!" Billy's command set her off like a gazelle in flight.

A cheer went up at the sight of Debra Warrington, and dozens of black, brown, and white hands reached out to touch her and wish her well. The Africans were laughing, shouting, and slapping each other's hands. The whites tended to be more reserved, but several men and women hugged and some had tears running down their cheeks. Billy saw even big, tough Fernando Singh dabbing watery eyes.

Debra made straight for the front door, from which an officer emerged carrying a small bundle.

"My baby! My baby!"

She swept the child from the officer's outstretched arms, setting off a new explosion of celebration. The little face inside the printed cloth looked swollen and pocked with insect bites, but it was her Dominic, all right! His blue eyes awakened in recognition, and Debra nuzzled his cheek.

"Two boys found him hidden in some tall grass down at the swamp," said the officer. "Good thing they came along. He could have died out there."

"Thank you... Thank all of you."

Debra started sobbing again. Her big, happy tears triggered another burst of cheers, clapping, and dancing. Through the noise, Debra heard a whimper.

"You must be so hungry, little man. Let's find a place where I can feed you."

Billy led them to his Combi. Debra removed the sodden and filthy cloth from the child and dumped it on the ground before entering the relative privacy of the vehicle. In less than two minutes Dominic found what he needed most—his mother's comforting, nourishing breast.

There was movement behind him, and Billy noticed Scott's red Cruiser approach. The swirling mass of joyful humanity made way as soon as they recognized him, all except for one especially animated clique that was so caught up in their dancing that they were oblivious to his presence. Billy quickly took over the role of traffic police.

"Just leave the Cruiser here. I'll get your chair."

"Where is Dominic? Is he OK?"

"He's with Debra in my Combi. She's nursing him. He is badly bitten and dirty, but seems OK. I'll take you there."

People had formed a tight circle around the Combi, but they made a path to let Billy and Scott pass. Scott sat too low to look through the windows. Billy tapped at the window to alert Debra that Scott was there. He then slid the door back far enough to allow Scott an unrestricted view.

Scott felt like melting as he spotted Dominic, wedged against Debra's breast, feasting his body and soul on the nourishment and security only his mother could give him. The child's eyes were locked on Debra's face, relaxed and peaceful. Debra, too, seemed indifferent to a care in the world. She looked up at Scott and smiled at him, communicating peace, love, and tremendous pride. He lingered several minutes, savoring the intimacy. Then he blew her kisses and gently closed the door. He pushed his chair back against the crowd and turned it around. Everybody watched him intently.

"This is the biggest miracle ever," he stated, using the back of his hands to wipe tears off his cheeks. "I'll tell the whole world. Only God could have brought Dominic back alive."

As he struggled to turn his chair around, a hush fell on the crowd. Scott cut through it. "Billy, how did they find him?"

Before Billy had uttered a word, a cheer went up. He looked up and saw Irina and Valerie pushing through the crowd toward them. Irina was both laughing and crying. She embraced Scott, Billy, and Valerie. More friends and volunteers pressed in, starting another round of hugging, laughing, and crying. African women ululated, men clapped, youngsters cheered. The excitement was infectious.

"Where is he?" Irina asked.

Scott pointed to the VW Combi. She walked over and peered in, shielding her eyes against the morning light reflecting off the window. She gazed at the baby Debra was nursing.

"He is dirty and covered in red spots, but this is the baby I gave birth to, my child," she whispered.

Valerie gently placed her arm around Irina.

Irina spun around and leaped in the air. "He's alive! My baby is alive. I am so happy!" She danced in circles and hugged Valerie, Billy, and Scott once more.

Suddenly Scott's expression changed from elation to concern. "Valerie, we need a medical doctor to check out Dominic. See if you can get through to the Keas. Mike is a pediatrician, and his wife is an orthopedic surgeon. Maybe both will examine Dominic this morning."

Valerie wasted no time dialing the Keas's number. As she waited for them to answer, the shouts of joy and dancing continued around her.

chapter 71
BACK IN THE HEADLINES

ONDAWAN NATIONAL RADIO broke the news that Dominic Warrington had been found and returned to his parents. The news swept across Mondawa like a giant tsunami wave. It was shouted from house to house, shop to shop, and field to field, on busses, bicycles, and through the bush.

Everywhere it went, the news triggered wild celebration. It caused pandemonium in the capital city as people shouted, danced, and cried with joy. Traffic jammed for several hours as droves of people exited their cars to discuss the good news. Vendors dropped prices, adding fuel to the party spirit.

"Warrington Baby Found Safe" declared the banner headline in Wednesday morning's *The Mondawa Times*. The newspaper then gave this summary report:

> On Saturday morning, 15 February, the fourteen-month-old son of Scott and Debra Warrington was violently kidnapped from his home in Kasiki. Members of the community turned out in great numbers to participate in the search for the kidnappers and the child.
>
> Shortly before midnight on Monday, two young men returning from a tavern decided to investigate a whimpering sound in a swamp they were passing. They expected to find a snared animal but found a white baby instead. They took the child to the village headman, who carried the baby to the police station a few hours later.
>
> The Warringtons were notified early Tuesday morning and rushed to the police station, where they were reunited with their adopted child. Also present was the boy's biological mother, who is a friend of the Warringtons. Doctors who examined the baby said he was reasonably well, apart from signs of dehydration and neglect. As a precautionary measure,

young Dominic was treated for malaria, as he had suffered hundreds of insect bites.

A special thanksgiving service was held on the same day. The Kasiki church couldn't accommodate the large number of people attending. A cross-section of society, including Christians, Muslims, Hindus, agnostics, blacks, whites, Asians, and coloureds, attended the service, which was led by Rev. Billy Summer. The reverend spoke about the biblical story of Jonah, who spent three days and three nights in the belly of a huge fish. He reminded those present that on the day after the kidnapping, the search for Dominic had been named "Operation Jonah."

He then posed the question, "Was it merely a strange coincidence that, like Jonah, Dominic was returned to his family three nights and almost three days after a harrowing ordeal? When I look into your faces I know you agree with me that this was God answering prayer."

The two young men who found the child, Abubakar Nkhomo and William Zulu are due to receive a reward of 150,000 Kwanzos. The identity and whereabouts of the two kidnappers is still being investigated. Authorities in South Africa report that the biological father is being charged with conspiracy to kidnap.

EPILOGUE
Debra's Reflections

M ANY YEARS LATER, people still approach us. "Are you not the family that...?" We still tend to hold our breath as to the second part of the sentence.

Even though we were largely unaware that the courts had considered but subsequently denied the right of the biological father to adopt his own son, we felt blamed for it. It was hard living with public and legal opinion that, until the kidnapping, was strongly critical of our right to bring up Dominic as our own son.

After the shock of kidnapping, I was an emotional wreck. It didn't help that we feared another kidnapping attempt. We never returned to live in our home in Kasiki. The kidnapping tested and reaffirmed our right and resolve to fight for Dominic's interests as typical parents would. The test was gut-wrenching. Each day of Dominic's absence I begged God that he would be returned that day. But then it would get dark and cold, and I felt choked by misery and despair. God gave us little signs along the way to encourage us, things to hold on to—like when I heard someone had coined the name for the search "Operation Jonah." Thinking of Jonah in the whale raised my hopes. Yet, my prayers were frantic. "Please, God, let him not be gone for longer than three days!"

Dominic was back in my arms three hours short of the three days!

Now when people approach us and say, "Are you not the family that...?" they are excited Dominic was found in time and returned relatively unharmed. Without completing the first sentence, they usually jump into the next: "We prayed so much for you when it happened."

We feel it was the prayers of hundreds of people around the world that helped us get Dominic back, and that people volunteered their time, sleep, and resources. One business gave up their radio and newspaper advertising slots for appeals for information regarding Dominic and for reward notices.

And Dominic? Immediately following his ordeal, he chomped through eight king prawns in one sitting, plus one and a half packets of Marie biscuits. Within days he recovered from a setback in his motor skills. Gradually, the nightmares that disturbed his sleep subsided. Today he only knows from stories what happened to him.

Abubakar Nkhomo and his friend William spent their reward before they were linked to the kidnappers. Anthony Castledyn was jailed in South Africa until bail was posted. He appealed the ruling of the criminal court and was allowed to convert his sentence into community service. The kidnappers served time in jail. Silver and a number of his thugs died in mysterious circumstances.

The kidnapping, though horrific, deepened our faith in a miracle-working God who answered our prayers in spectacular ways. We liken our three days of agony while separated from Dominic with Christ's cruel death and, also after three days, His resurrection. We continue to be missionaries pursuing the dream of the whole world coming to know Christ as we do.

The end of a matter is better than its beginning.
—ECCLESIASTES 7:8

GLOSSARY

TERM	MEANING	LANGUAGE OR DIALECT
Asante sana	"Thank you"	Swahili
Baba/Bwana	A respectful term for "father," "sir," "mister," or "boss"	Bantu
Bakkie	Small utility truck or pickup	Afrikaans
Boerewors	South African beef sausage	Afrikaans
Braai	Barbeque	Afrikaans
Coloureds	A non-derogatory term for people of mixed African/European race	
Cow-catcher	A crude grill, mainly on off-road vehicles, to protect the front of a car against the impact of animals	
Highveld	The high-plateau region of South Africa, of which Johannesburg is a part	
Odi	"Hello, may I come in?"	Bantu
Odini	"Come in. You are welcome."	Bantu
Marie biscuits	A common brand of South African cookie	
Muti	African medicine	
NoiseBoys	Franchised car mechanics	
Roti	Indian type of bread	
Recce	A term used for the South African Special Forces during the South African border war	
Samoosa	Fried triangular-shaped pastry with a savory filling	
Ululation	A long, high-pitched, wordless sound expressing jubilation or grief. It is also an integral part of most weddings, where people ululate to welcome the groom or bride or both.	